Two sets of lovers...
Will history repeat itself?

Raymond Giovanni Sandetti: Fif[...] ago he fell in love with Janet [...] Christmas Eve. A [...] [...] [...]k for her—bu[...] and he wasn[...] [...] successful bu[...] the worst mist[...] [...] placed ambition over [...]

Janet Fridrich: When she was a love-struck teenager, Ray had been everything to her. But their love had frightened her, especially when it meant giving up everything she'd ever known. Married and widowed, she's never forgotten Ray.

Nicholas Ciminero: Ray's surrogate son, Nick is driven by his past. Having grown up in a series of orphanages, he doesn't trust love and family. He's determined to not need anyone.

Sarah McGrath: She's never met a man like Nick, but for her, family has to come first. And she's afraid that if Nick learns the shocking truth about her past, she'll lose him forever.

Dear Reader,

We have a special treat for you this month, plus lots of exciting news about 1994. Kristine Rolofson wrote the very first Lovers & Legends title, a contemporary treatment of *Snow White and the Seven Dwarfs*. It's only fitting that she also conclude the series with a Christmas story. She picked a much more modern tale, Dickens's *A Christmas Carol*, and has neatly woven love stories from Christmas Past, Present and Future. *I'll Be Seeing You* is a lovely, romantic book that made more than one editor cry!

Popular Leandra Logan has also written a wonderful Christmas story, *Joyride*. Longtime favorites JoAnn Ross and Gina Wilkins round out this holiday month.

1994 is going to be full of excitement—Temptation celebrates its tenth anniversary. To begin, we have Passion's Quest. *Earth, wind, fire, water... the four elements—but nothing is more elemental than passion.* One book a month, from January to April, will be an adventure story revolving around one of the elements—*Body Heat* by Elise Title, *Wild Like the Wind* by Janice Kaiser, *Aftershock* by Lynn Michaels and *Undercurrent* by Lisa Harris. Four fantastic adventure stories, four fantastic love stories, in the tradition of *Romancing the Stone* and *The African Queen*.

We'll have other surprises in 1994 as well! Happy reading.

Birgit Davis-Todd

Senior Editor

I'll Be Seeing You

Kristine Rolofson

Harlequin Books

TORONTO • NEW YORK • LONDON
AMSTERDAM • PARIS • SYDNEY • HAMBURG
STOCKHOLM • ATHENS • TOKYO • MILAN
MADRID • WARSAW • BUDAPEST • AUCKLAND

For my father, Don Winslow HMC USN (Ret.),
1st MAR DIV, 2nd Bn 7th, C Med,
whose memories inspired this story,

And my mother, Ottis Winslow,
who declared this "the best book yet"
before she'd read it.

And special thanks to Nancy and Ned Mack
for letting me borrow their beautiful home
in North Platte.

ISBN 0-373-25569-1

I'LL BE SEEING YOU

Copyright © 1993 by Kristine Rolofson.

1

December 24, 1942

"NORTH PLATTE coming up," the conductor called. "You'll have fifteen minutes! Better make the most of it!"

Ray Sandetti shifted his long legs as the train lurched and slowed down. The dark car was cold and his feet were numb, despite the regulation navy shoes he wore. He shivered. There'd been no heat since west of New York. Ray wondered if, when they finally reached California, the marine unit he was joining would be transferred to the South Pacific. Some of that jungle sun would feel good right about now.

But shipping out to the South Pacific was just a rumor, and the train was as full of rumors as it was servicemen. Ray looked at his watch. Three o'clock in the morning and he felt as if he'd been on this train for weeks instead of days. He stretched his legs in front of him as much as he could, then attempted to wipe the window so he could see what the area was like. All he could see was snow.

The kid next to him leaned forward to look. "Hey, Sandy! Where are we?"

Ray shrugged. "Somewhere in the Midwest called North Platte. Does it matter?"

"Well, yeah." Jerry grinned. "It's Christmas Eve. I like to know where I'm spending Christmas Eve, don't you?"

"I don't care." Ray shrugged, hoping his homesickness didn't show. "Guess if I'm not home, it doesn't matter." He turned back to the window, although there wasn't much to see but a few vague lights through the darkness. It sure didn't feel like Christmas. Mama would have the tree decorated by now, and the turkey would be ready to put into the oven. And the lasagna. He could almost taste the sauce. Her last letter said she and Rosa were saving sugar rations so they'd have enough for the cookies. Papa would be playing the radio and waiting for war news.

There was always war news.

The train lurched and brakes squealed, until the train stopped. Jerry stood up and buttoned his coat. "We're in luck stopping in North Platte. Man, I've heard about this place. You can put your meal tickets away. They *give* us food. Real food."

Ray didn't have to be told twice. He grabbed his cap and stumbled off the train with the rest of the passengers. He pulled up the collar of his thick peacoat and kept his head down, trying to protect his face from the fierce wind as he crossed the tracks to the depot and a hot cup of coffee. Anything hot sounded like one hell of a Christmas present.

The first thing he noticed was the women. The large lunchroom was loaded with them, and they were all working with food. Ray blinked against the bright light and inhaled the warm air. Did he smell turkey or was it his imagination?

"Line up, boys," one woman called, waving them toward a long table. "Haven't got much time! Better hurry!"

The plates were the familiar Blue Willow pattern of his childhood. He could picture his mother stacking them beside the sink and a lump filled Ray's throat. He shook his head. A homesick sailor on Christmas Eve was a pretty sad sight.

Jerry elbowed him. "Grab one of those sandwiches, Sandy. Man, oh, man, is this a sight? I think I've died and gone to heaven."

Copper platters held stacks of sandwiches, with homemade bread so thick they looked like triple-deckers. The tables were decorated with shiny glass bulbs and red bows tied onto branches of evergreen. Fat round pitchers of milk stood off to one end, surrounded by fat white coffee cups. Hard-boiled eggs, cakes, and platters of cookies filled the tables and Ray moved down the line, helping himself to a generous meal before reaching the end.

"Merry Christmas!"

Ray looked up to see a young girl holding a heavy pitcher. Blue eyes, yellow hair and the prettiest smile he'd ever seen greeted him.

"Thank you," he muttered, although he didn't know how he managed to get the words out. *Wholesome* was the first thing he thought as he looked at her. She was everything normal. Peaches and cream. Peaceful days without war talk. Nights without worrying about dying. "Merry Christmas to you, too."

The color in her cheeks heightened as he stared at her. "Coffee or milk?"

Ray tore his gaze away, but only for a second. "Milk, for now."

"Here," she said, handing him a cup. "There's plenty, if you have time to drink it."

"Thanks." Ray wondered if she'd milked the cows herself. He would believe it, would believe anything after dropping into this warm room after the frozen eternity on the train. He looked behind him and realized he was the last person in line. "Who are you?"

"Janet." She smiled. "I live here."

He looked at her left hand. No wedding ring. These days you never knew, since couples were getting married so young. "Can you talk to me while I eat?"

Janet looked around and seemed satisfied that she had a few moments of freedom. "Okay." She led him to a couple of empty chairs in a corner and sat down before he could pull out a chair for her.

"Tell me about this place." *Tell me all about you.*

"What do you want to know?"

"Anything. I just want to hear your voice." Ray picked up his sandwich and bit into it hungrily.

Janet's cheeks once again grew pink. "Why?"

"Because you're the most beautiful girl I've ever seen. Do all the girls in Nebraska look like you?"

Janet started to stand up. "I think I'd better go help—"

"I'm sorry," Ray said, and meant it with all his heart. "I won't embarrass you any more, I promise." He hurried to think of something to talk about that wouldn't make her leave. "Tell me about North Platte and where all this food comes from."

"Okay." She sat back down. "The Union Pacific railroad lets us use the lunchroom. Groups from all over this part of Nebraska take turns meeting the trains and making the meals. It's our contribution to the war effort."

"Well, this sailor appreciates it."

"I'm glad." She looked pleased. "Where are you headed? Do you know?"

"I'm a navy medic, going to join the marines." Ray shook his head. He didn't want to talk about the war. "How old are you?"

"Sixteen."

"Have a boyfriend?"

Her eyes twinkled. "I thought you wanted to hear about North Platte."

He wondered how a woman could look so beautiful at three o'clock in the morning. "You're still in high school, right?"

She nodded. "I'm a junior."

"I'll bet you're a cheerleader."

"No."

"Live on a farm?"

"Wrong again, sailor. I live right here in town."

"Will you write to me?"

"I don't even know you."

"Raymond Giovanni Sandetti. From Providence, Rhode Island."

"Rhode Island. Is that in New York?"

"No. *Long* Island is part of New York. Rhode Island is the smallest state in the union. It's on the Atlantic coast."

"I've never seen the ocean," she admitted. "I've always wanted to."

"We're headed for the Pacific, I think. I guess I'm going to see a lot of it."

"My brother is somewhere in Europe," she said. "My mother watches for the mailman every day."

Ray nodded grimly. "I'll bet my mother does the same thing. And my father, too. My mother can't believe the navy wouldn't let me come home for Christmas." He grinned at the beautiful girl across the table. "And neither can I."

"I would hate that," she said. "I would be so homesick—" She broke off. "I'm sorry. That wasn't very thoughtful of me."

"It's okay." Ray wanted to see her smile again. He lifted the last piece of sandwich. "You gave me a great Christmas dinner."

"I'm glad." The smile returned, and Ray figured the temperature in the room went up ten degrees. "Have you ever eaten a lobster? I've read about lobster."

"You have?"

"I read all the time," she admitted.

"I'll write to you." Ray put his empty plate on the floor and pulled a pen from his coat pocket. He found the letter he'd started to his mother and tore off the corner. "Here." He held out the paper and pen. "Will you give me your address?"

She shook her head and didn't take the paper he offered. "It's against the rules."

"Then take mine." He scribbled his address on the scrap of paper and held it out to her, but she didn't accept it.

"Well, maybe it would—"

"Janet!"

They both looked up as a tiny woman waved in their direction. "My mother," Janet explained. "She let me stay up and help tonight because it's Christmas Eve. I have to go now or she won't let me help again."

She stood and so did Ray. He put one hand on her arm, barely restraining her with his fingers. "Write to me, Janet. I'll write back. And I'll come back here when the war is over and ask you to marry me. We'll have kids who swim in the ocean and eat lobster."

She didn't pull away, but touched his fingers lightly with her own before she turned and hurried toward her mother. Ray watched as the women passed out popcorn balls and desserts wrapped in waxed paper.

"Three minutes," someone called. "All aboard in three minutes!"

Ray couldn't take his gaze off her. He liked the way she moved, liked the yellow streaks in her hair and the light in her blue eyes. He knew now why men did crazy things where women were concerned. He felt pretty crazy himself right now. She looked back at him, to see if he was watching her, and he didn't look away as her cheeks flushed when she realized he'd caught her.

Raymond felt a tug on his sleeve and turned to see Jerry holding a sack. "Hey, pal. Time to climb aboard. I got a bag of cookies to take with us. They're giving away cakes, too, if it's anyone's birthday." He looked at Ray with a hopeful expression. "Is it your birthday?"

"No." He watched as Janet approached him, a popcorn ball in her hand. "But it *is* my lucky day."

She held it out to him. "Merry Christmas, Raymond Giovanni Sandetti."

"Write to me," he urged as the train whistle blew impatiently.

"Take it," she said, pressing the dessert into his hand. "Make sure you eat every bite."

Popcorn was the last thing Ray cared about. He wanted the little blond teenager in the plaid cotton dress to tell him what he wanted to hear. "I'm coming back for you," he promised. "Don't marry anyone else until you see me again."

"I won't."

He took one last look over his shoulder as Jerry pulled him away. "Promise?" he called.

"Promise."

It would have to be enough for now, Ray decided. He shivered against the wind blowing snow into his face and ran to the train as it began its slow chugging along the tracks. Once on board, he found his seat and looked out the frosted window to see the train station of North Platte disappear behind a cloud of snow. A few multi-colored Christmas lights in the distance were soon the only things he could see, and he leaned back against the seat with a sigh. He sure as hell didn't know where he'd end up, but he'd remember this night for the rest of his life.

"You gonna eat that?" Jerry stretched next to him.

Ray looked down to see that he still held the popcorn ball. He'd almost forgotten. "Yes," he answered, still huddled in his coat. "I promised I would."

"She was sure a pretty girl."

"Yeah." She was the most beautiful girl he'd ever seen. Ray unwrapped the waxed paper with careful fingers, and the ball split in half as he released it from its wrapping. "Damn, it broke!"

Jerry looked over, interested. "If you don't want it, I'll eat it."

Ray ignored him as he looked at two halves of the popcorn ball and a tiny piece of paper. He picked it up and read the girlish handwriting. "Janet Fridrich, West 4th Street." Ray smiled and tucked the paper into his wallet. Janet Fridrich would be hearing from him very soon. He was a man who kept his promises.

"MAMA WOULD HAVE a fit," Mary Anne announced, her hands on her hips. "You know she would."

"Because I got a letter?"

"You're not supposed to give your address to the servicemen. It's against the rules."

"Oh, pooh. Lots of girls put their addresses inside the popcorn balls, or write them in magazines. The boys like magazines."

"Mama wouldn't like it."

"So don't tell her." Janet smiled at her younger sister. Mary Anne was fourteen, two years younger than herself, but she tried desperately to act older. Even if that meant trying to boss her older sister around. "If I get in trouble, who's going to take you places? Mama will never let you go alone."

Her sister flopped on the bed, defeated. "I wish *I* could work at the canteen after school sometimes."

"You can't be a platform girl unless you're sixteen."

"But it must be so much fun to run up and down next to the train and give all those cute boys magazines and candy. Patty Smith told me that sometimes you give toothbrushes, too."

"I've never seen them," Janet said, staring at the envelope in her hand.

"'North Platte, Nebraska,' is printed on the side. Why would anyone want a toothbrush with 'North Platte' on it? There's nothing to do here." She rolled onto her stomach, tucked a pillow under her chin, and stared at her older sister. "I wish I could get a letter from a sailor. Aren't you gonna open it?"

"In a minute." Strong, slanted handwriting. Blue ink. "When you stop chattering and go away."

"I can't watch?"

Janet looked over at her sister and relented. She wished she had her own room, but Mama wouldn't let anyone move into Robert's bedroom and she'd quit asking because it made her mother cry. But the mailman had brought a letter from him today and Mama would read it to everyone at the supper table tonight.

"You can sit here very quietly while I read it, but if you say *one word* I won't let you go to the market with me tomorrow."

"Okay. I'll be quiet, like a little mouse." Mary Anne made a zipping motion across her lips and settled onto the crushed pillow once again.

Satisfied, Janet carefully opened the V-mail and unfolded the flimsy sheet of paper that made its own envelope. Dark writing covered the page.

The letter read:

Dear Janet,

I'll bet you thought I wasn't going to write. I'll bet I surprised you. My unit is in California now, but I can't say where we'll be, even if I knew. I have a pretty good idea, though. They say we'll still get mail, so please write back. You don't know anything about me, I know, but if we write to each other we'd get to know each other, right? What did you do on Christmas? I thought about you that day. We were still on the train. North Platte was the only good stop on the whole trip. All the guys were talking about it. This place is okay. We don't have much free time, though. I wouldn't want to live here if I had a choice. Yesterday I met a guy from Nebraska, but he's never been to North Platte. I think he was from Omaha. I told him about meeting you, the most beautiful girl I've ever seen. He said you must have been my Christmas present. (I probably shouldn't have told you that, but it's too late now.) So write back and tell me about yourself and your family and school, okay?

Sincerely,
Raymond Sandetti

"You're smiling. Can I talk now?"

Janet folded the letter back up and looked over at her sister. "Yes."

"Who is he?"

"Ray Sandetti, from Rhode Island." She went over to her desk and slid the letter inside the top drawer. She'd answer it later, before she went to sleep. She'd have all evening to think of what she was going to write to the tall, dark-haired sailor with the beautiful dark eyes and the homesick smile.

"Why is he so special? Is he nicer than Jimmy?"

Janet shrugged and closed the drawer. "I can't explain it, Mary Anne. Something really wonderful happened when I saw him, something that I've never felt before. But I *knew* him, almost, and he looked at me like he knew me, too."

"Wow!"

A smaller version of Janet opened the bedroom door and peeked inside. "Mommy says you hafta come help with supper."

"Louella," Mary Anne warned, "you're not supposed to come in our room without knocking! I've told you and told you!"

Louella ignored her and turned her blue-eyed gaze on her oldest sister. "Mama says."

"Okay, Lou. We're coming." Janet followed her youngest sister out the door, and Mary Anne grumbled behind her.

"Just because she's the youngest she thinks she can do anything she wants."

"Mama got a letter from Robbie," Louella announced. "And she's gonna read it to us at supper."

"Well, I can't wait," Janet said. "Here, honey, let me fix that braid." Louella stopped and looked at her sister with adoring eyes while Janet quickly rebraided her hair. "There, now you're beautiful."

"Not as beautiful as you."

Janet smiled and descended the wide staircase behind her sisters. Raymond Sandetti thought she was beautiful, too. She didn't consider herself vain, but it was nice to have someone *think* she was beautiful, even if she wasn't.

"DEAR RAY," Janet wrote, sitting at her desk long after the rest of the family had gone to sleep. Mary Anne snored softly from under a tangle of quilts, but otherwise the house was quiet. "Your letter came today. Of course I'll write to you! It's very late here. I finished my homework." Janet frowned at the page. She shouldn't have mentioned homework. It sounded so childish. She crumpled the paper and tossed it in the trash.

"Dear Ray," she tried again. "Your letter came today. I was really surprised to hear from you. I guess this means you ate the popcorn ball! North Platte is really cold and we had more snow today." Now she sounded like the weatherman on the radio. Oh, well.

Where were you on Christmas Day? My brother Robbie is in the army, still in Europe somewhere, but we're not certain. He can't say much in his letters, but we're always so happy to hear from him. We have a bulletin board with a map of the world on it, and we keep track of where the boys are. Everyone in town spreads the word whenever there is news from the front. By the way, I have two sisters. Mary Anne is fourteen and Louella is seven. We all miss my brother. He took care of everything and made my mother laugh even when she didn't want to.

Janet paused and chewed the end of her pen. This letter wasn't very interesting, but she didn't know how to make it better without making things up. If she wrote about school she'd sound like a kid. Actually, *any-thing* she wrote would make her sound like a kid. "We go to the show whenever we can. Have you seen *Casablanca*? I liked *Woman of the Year*, too, because Katherine Hepburn is one of my favorite actresses. Who's yours? Christmas Eve was the first time I've ever worked at the canteen, because Mama thought I was too young. She said she'll let me help next time." *But I bet I won't meet anyone like you.* Janet yawned and quickly added, "If you write again I'll write back, I promise. Sincerely, Janet."

She slipped the letter inside an envelope, carefully copied Raymond's address and wrote FREE in the corner where the stamp would have been. She'd drop it in the mailbox on the way to school in the morning. Maybe the handsome sailor would remember her.

THE SIX WEEKS in San Diego were the hardest Ray had ever known. Here he was, a navy medic, training in the Marine Corps. They would be shipping out soon. Maybe as soon as tomorrow. No one had said anything, but they didn't have to. There were lots of rumors, but the message was the same. He curled up on his bunk and grabbed a pen. Every time he wrote to Janet, she answered right away. It didn't get any better than that.

Dear Janet,
Your letter cheered me up when I was having a real bad day here. I can't say enough about how much your letters mean to me. I knew when I met you

that you were special and I'm still sure of it. I don't know what happened to me that night (or morning, I guess) in December but when I saw you I knew I was crazy about you.

I don't know what's going to happen to my unit next. No one does, but we're leaving soon. That's all I can say. You might think I'm crazy for writing all this, but I wanted you to know that your letters are real important and I keep them all and read them over and over again. You don't have to be embarrassed about writing about school. I like to hear it. Did you pass your English test? Tell Mary Anne and Louella that I can't wait to meet them, either. Things are heating up where Robbie is, from what I hear. The news is full of it. Maybe this will be over soon. Rosa wrote to me yesterday and asked if I'd met any girls. I wrote back and told her about you. My folks are working hard in the store, but Rosa helps out a lot, even though she's only a kid. I'd better get some sleep while I still can. I know you're not "my girl" but I think of you that way. I hope you don't mind. Where's the picture you were going to send me?

> Forever yours,
> Ray

"THERE'S ANOTHER letter from that boy. I put it on the dining room table." Martha Fridrich untied her apron and slipped it over the back of a kitchen chair.

"Hi, Mama! And thanks." Janet, still wrapped up in her winter coat and scarf, hurried into the other room, her mother following.

"It's good to write to our boys. Everyone knows that. But you can't get serious about someone you only met for what? Fifteen minutes?"

Janet found the letter propped up against Great-aunt Aggie's silver candlesticks, the one and only family heirloom. "It's hard to explain. Ray's different from anyone else I've ever met."

"There's a war on, Janet. People are too hasty today, too rushed."

"It's hard not to be, not with the boys all off to war, or about to go." She picked up the letter, wondering if she should tear it open now or wait for the privacy of her room. Mary Anne had stayed after school for a dance committee meeting, so she would have the bedroom all to herself.

"Robbie hasn't written in a week."

"If he's in Italy then we know he's very busy," Janet said gently. She tried to sound cheerful, but talking about Robbie had become pretty scary. The whole family knew he must be in the middle of heavy fighting. The newspaper was full of it, and the reports from that front weren't encouraging. She turned and gave her mother a hug. "Don't worry. He'd hate it if he knew you were so upset."

"I know," came her mother's muffled answer. She pulled back and wiped her eyes with her fingers. "I'm better now," she said, trying to smile. "I baked cinnamon rolls to have with supper. You go read your letter."

Janet didn't have to be told again. She grinned, and took the stairs two at a time.

Dear Ray,
Aren't you surprised to get so many letters?

Sometimes I feel like writing every day, so I do.
Yes, I do my homework first (sometimes!!!) so
don't think about that anymore. March is a very
long month here. There isn't much to do, except
wait for war news. My brother hasn't sent a letter
in weeks, and my mother is very sad and trying to
be brave. We took her to the show on Saturday.
She likes Westerns. Our sisters sound alike, don't
they? Tell Rosa she will have to come to Nebraska
some day and meet Mary Anne. I've heard your
division is in the Pacific now. Be very, very careful so you can come back to Nebraska some day,
okay?

I'm glad you liked the picture. It's from last year,
but I don't think I've changed very much. I heard
a song that made me think of you. "I'll Be Seeing
You." It's on the radio a lot.

My favorite color is blue and my birthday is June
16. Do you have any more questions? (You haven't
answered mine, remember?) I don't have a steady
boyfriend and I don't go out on dates very much,
but I keep busy! I sing in the church choir, go out
with my girlfriends (and boys too!!) and I write
letters to you and Robbie. Does that answer your
question??? Write back when you can.

                                          Always,
                                          Janet

March 1943:

Peaches (when I first saw you I thought of peaches
and cream, so that is my nickname for you), it's
pretty bad here. They read all our mail before they

send it out so I can't say much about where we are but I wish we were somewhere else. They keep me busy, if that tells you how it is. Is your mother any better? I answered Louella's letter yesterday. She must be a cute kid. Mail is <u>real</u> important here, more than food, more than anything. Getting a letter keeps us going so don't stop writing <u>no matter what</u>. I wish I was one of those guys sitting beside you at the movies and dancing with you and hearing you sing in church. I get jealous just thinking about it, and I know it's not right. But I really care about you—A LOT—and I keep telling myself that you might care about me too, or you wouldn't write like you do. You would have stopped by now. Do you care? I really think I fell in love with you the first moment I saw you. It hit me that hard. I didn't even know if I could talk. Do you believe in love at first sight? I do now. If you don't want me to write like this anymore I won't, but after all these months of writing I just had to tell you how I feel. I don't even know your middle name.

If you don't hear from me for a while, don't worry. We're moving around a lot, but they tell us we'll still get mail. It just might take longer. I carry V-mail blanks with me, so I can write when I get a chance.

All my love,
Ray

"Medic!"
Ray peered out of the foxhole. "Coming!" He tucked the letter inside his jacket and snapped his helmet. He

felt good, as if he'd spent the past thirty minutes talk-ing to Janet. *His* Janet. Someday he would see her again. Everyone said this war couldn't last forever.

2

April 11, 1943

Dear Ray,

The daffodils are blooming. I wish I could send you one. Next month we'll have lilacs from the big bush in the backyard. We hear of the fighting in the Pacifie, and all the news of Guadalcanal. I keep thinking and worrying about you, and I look for your face on the newsreels. I haven't seen you yet! But I wouldn't know what you looked like with your helmet on, would I?

We've taken in a boarder, a schoolteacher, for extra money. Mama put her in Robbie's room. She'll be staying through the summer and next school year, too. Mama is happy because she heard from Rob yesterday. There's no news about when he'll come home, of course. He's been better about writing but of course we don't know where he is unless we hear news of the 7th on the radio.

I wish I could see you again, and I know I will someday. I don't know what to think about the night we met, but I feel as if I know you after reading your letters for so many months. You are very special to me, Raymond Giovanni Sandetti, and I want you to stay safe and come home soon. I still have your Valentine on my mirror in the corner where I look at it every morning when I curl my hair.

Mary Anne, Mama and I worked at the canteen yesterday. The trains were full of servicemen, and I wished so much that you were one of them, just so I could see you again. I don't know if what we have is love. So many crazy things are happening in this war. Love happens so fast and people seem so desperate. I don't want us to be desperate. When I love someone I want it to be forever, and I don't want it to be because of the war.

You are my special and dear Ray, and I can't wait to see you again.

With love,
Janet

Hi, Peaches!

You'll never guess where I am. I guess I'm allowed to tell you we're doing Australian duty, which isn't too tough to take, especially after the last months. It was so hot on G. that some days were like walking barefoot on hot coals. The Aussies are great. They opened up their homes to let us stay with them, and they treat us real good. We eat a lot of mutton, so I may never want to eat it again! Melbourne is a beautiful city, with stores, bars, hotels, soda fountains and thousands of real friendly people. There are lots of white beaches, and farmland, too. (Maybe Nebraska looks a little like this.) It looks a lot like home, or what I remember home to be. At last, I feel like we're back in civilization.

There's been a few fist fights with the Aussie 9th Division, in fact, quite a lot. We had a beer party, to try to settle things down. Nine thousand guys drank beer out of paper cups (so we wouldn't throw the bottles at each other). I've never thrown a bottle at anyone, but I sure can hold my own in a fight. A Sandetti doesn't back down. Now we play football and they play rugby and you wouldn't believe how crazy a combination it is! We call it "Austus."

One more funny thing: the girls don't believe we don't have false teeth! Lots of people, young people, here have them.

I think about home all the time. I try not to, because it drives me crazy to think of my family all being together and I'm not there. Rosa writes almost every day and tells me about school. My mother's English isn't too good, so she mostly sends messages through Rosa, which works just fine. The store is doing okay and they have enough to eat.

I live for your letters. One of my buddies saw your picture (the first one you sent me) and said "Wow, where'd you meet a girl like that?" I told him he wouldn't believe me, and he didn't. He said he hopes to go through North Platte when he ships out, just to see if there are any more girls like you. I told him I have the best one.

I think we'll be here for a while. I guess the Old Man wants to get us ready for the next big one. For now we're all having a good time and we're real happy to be here. The last few months have been h---. I feel real glad to be alive and here in Melbourne.

I'll be seeing you.

All my love,
Ray

Dear Ray,
I thought of you so much today. Can you believe it's been almost a year since we met? Did you get the Christmas package? I followed all the directions on how to mail packages, so I hope it found you, wherever you

are. New Year's Eve is only a week away, and then it will be 1944. Maybe this will be the year the war ends and you will come home.

I love the bracelet you sent and I will wear it every day. It's special because it came from Melbourne and from you! Thank you for such a beautiful surprise.

School is keeping me very busy. There are lots of papers to write, and we've been making quilts to send to Britain. Mama's been knitting socks in the evening when we listen to our favorite shows.

We put up a very small tree this year. Somehow it doesn't seem right to celebrate without Rob. I'm sure your mother and father feel the same way without you, too, but we're all being very strong and very brave and doing our best to keep everything going well here.

"I'll Be Seeing You," too.

Love and Merry Christmas,
Janet

Peaches,
There's not much time. We're getting ready for something big. No matter what, just remember that sailor who fell in love with you last Christmas Eve, please? Don't forget me, and don't forget your promise.

Gary Cooper was here (I can't say where) last night. He said, "Get those SOBs for me!" I couldn't believe that Coop would swear. They showed movies, which helped us calm down.

No more time, don't forget me, ever.

All my love,
Ray

"NO MAIL?"

Martha Fridrich shook her head. She wished she

could have answered differently. There had been no word for weeks from Ray, and Janet suffered more than she would have thought possible. They were all worried, for with his frequent letters Raymond Sandetti had become almost a member of the family.

Janet blinked back tears. "He's in the middle of all that fighting, I just know it."

Martha put her arm around her oldest daughter and hugged her. "You keep writing, honey. That's all you can do."

"I know I didn't know him at first, but we've been writing for so long now. We tell each other everything."

"You have to be strong. For all you know, he's getting his mail and reading your letters every day. He probably doesn't have any control over sending mail to you."

"He always has before," Janet countered, wiping her eyes.

"What do you tell me when I don't hear from your brother?"

"'Never give up hope.'"

Martha smiled. "You listen to your own advice, young lady. And go write that young man a cheerful letter."

"Dear Ray," she began, seated at her desk as the last of the late-afternoon sun shone in her room. "I had an English test today..."

Dear Janet,
I'm sorry I haven't written lately. It's wet here, so wet that our clothes never dry out. Not EVER. I'm real glad to be alive, but I'll be even gladder to get out of this

d--- place. My pocketknife has rusted and my boots are moldy. I've been thinking a lot about my mother's cooking. The food in Rhode Island is wonderful, especially at our market. I sit in my foxhole, wrapped up in my poncho, and dream of what I will do in the market when this war is over. I'm thinking pretty big things, sitting here in a hole full of mud and land crabs!

Don't send any pictures for a while. They just rot. Your letters only last a day before they fall apart. My waterproof watch is covered with mold and doesn't work anymore. That's the first thing I'm going to do when I get stateside duty—is buy a new watch. One that won't rot in the jungle, because I'm never coming back here again, not if this guy has anything to say about it!

Thanks again for the presents. I shared your Christmas package with the other guys. Hope you don't mind, that's what we do here. I didn't know I was falling in love with such a good cook. You're sure full of surprises.

Are you going out with other boys? It makes me crazy to think of it, but I have no hold on you. I know you need to go out and I want you to, because you should have a lot of dates before you marry me. I want you to be sure about me.

Hey, Peaches, I won't be serious any longer, okay? Smile for me and don't forget your promise. Don't marry anyone else. Don't forget, you have to give me a chance first.

All my love forever,
Ray

Dear Ray,
Can you believe that your Janet is now a high school

graduate? I thought I would feel very grown-up and very old—and I do! Even if my 19th birthday is only a few weeks away! Dr. Johnson offered me a job in his office, so I will be a secretary in a few days. I'm to answer the phone and make appointments. Doesn't that sound perfect? I was afraid I would have to move to Lincoln or Omaha to find work, which some of my girlfriends are doing. But I love it here, and Mama needs me.

We took the bus to Lincoln last weekend and went shopping. We have cousins there, so we stayed with them. It was so good for Mama to have a small vacation, and the rest of us didn't mind it either!

Mary Anne is dating three boys at once. She has turned into quite a beauty. Wait till you meet her! Lou is still sweet and shy, but she is growing up. I think of your sister often, and wonder if she is doing the same things our Lou-Lou does!

Your "rest camp" sounds terrible (I can read between the lines, you know, no matter how you try to cover it up) and I hope you are gone from there soon. Nebraska is so dry. It's hard to believe there are places in the world where it rains all the time.

You asked me about my father, and I'm not sure what you wanted to know. I think you would have liked him. He was a very quiet man who worked for the railroad. My mother talks about him all the time, so she has kept his memory alive for us. She is always so brave and strong. I wish I was more like her.

I would NEVER break a promise, cross my heart. I go out sometimes, but there is no one "special" person—not unless you count Raymond Sandetti! If there was someone else, I would tell you. I miss you very much, and wish we could be together to talk to each other. I love your letters, but I would love to know the person you are even more. I DO love you, Ray. Sometimes I wonder what would have happened if I'd never met you that night, and that frightens me. Your letters help so much. I don't know what I'd do if I didn't have them to look forward to. I don't know what will happen to us after the war is over, but for now . . .

Love,
Janet

JANET PUT DOWN her pen and carefully folded the letter and tucked it inside the envelope. Sometimes it was so hard to stay cheerful, but everyone said don't send the boys bad news, or complain about life back home. An article in the *Ladies' Home Journal* cautioned against writing letters when you were feeling sad, but sometimes that was hard to do. This month's *Saturday Evening Post* cover showed a soldier opening his mail and finding his new baby's bootees. Just looking at the picture had made her want to cry, but Miss Hester had been in the living room, too, so indulging herself in a good cry couldn't happen.

"Janet, will you fix my hair?"

"Sure, sweetheart." Louella entered the room while Janet quickly sealed the envelope and propped it against her lamp. "Do you have your brush?"

The child nodded. "Are you writing to Ray again?"

Janet started brushing the tangled honey-colored hair, working her fingers carefully through the tangles. "Yes. He likes to get letters."

"Where is he?"

"I think he's still in the Pacific. He can't tell me, but I think he's fighting on one of those other jungle islands."

"Is he your boyfriend?"

"Sort of."

"Are you going to marry him when the war is over and move far, far away?"

Janet paused and turned the child around so she could look at her. "Why would you say that?"

"Mary Anne said."

"Don't look so worried, honey. I'm not going anywhere." She tapped her on the nose. "Mary Anne just likes to think I'm going to leave."

"Why?"

"Because then she'd have this room all to herself." Janet took Louella's shoulders and turned her back around. "Let's finish your hair. I think I have all the tangles out. How many braids do you want? One? Two? Six? Twenty?"

The child giggled. "One."

"Well, *that's* easy enough. You'll be beautiful in no time."

"Not as beautiful as you!"

"Not as beautiful as *you!*" They both laughed at the old routine, but Janet wondered at Lou's question. *Would* she marry Ray? It was a possibility, of course. How could she imagine life without having Ray to "talk" to? She didn't know how her life had become so entwined with Ray's, and yet she wasn't surprised. The night they met was still sharp and clear in her memory, as if it were yesterday. She knew something special had happened, but she didn't know where it would lead. This hateful war had to end first.

"WHERE IS IT?"

"I put it under the tree."

Janet stepped into the living room and found a small parcel addressed to her and postmarked Providence, Rhode Island. She picked it up and looked at her mother. "What do you think it is?"

Martha smiled. "You'll have to open it to find out. It must be from Ray's parents."

Mary Anne chimed in, "Or Ray had them send you something from him."

"He didn't say anything about it."

"Of course not, silly. It's supposed to be a surprise. After all, it's Christmas, isn't it?"

Martha smiled at her daughters. "I don't suppose you're going to wait until tomorrow to open it?"

Janet was already untying the string as Louella edged closer. "Of course not." She tossed the string aside, unwrapped the brown paper from the box, and pried open the flaps. Above the crumpled paper lay a sealed envelope, addressed to her in Ray's handwriting.

"What is it?" Mary Anne stepped closer.

"I don't know yet," Janet answered. "I think I should read the letter first."

"Yes," Martha said. "I think so, too."

Janet opened the envelope and unfolded a sheet of paper. "Merry Christmas, darling!" she read silently.

I wish with all of my heart I could give this to you in person, but we both know that's impossible. I'm not asking you to say yes right now, but when I return to you and ask you to marry me, I want you to have had plenty of time to think about how much I love you and how much you mean to me. All I ask is that you look at it once in a while and think about me.

With all my love,
Ray

With trembling fingers Janet put down the letter and lifted the bunch of paper to reveal a velvet jewelry box. She lifted it up and opened the lid. A diamond ring twinkled at her from its black velvet bed. "Oh, my goodness," she breathed. "I can't believe this!"

Martha peered over her shoulder. "It's beautiful, but if you put that on your finger you'd best be very certain that's what you want."

"Oh, I'm certain, all right." Janet didn't hesitate. She took the ring and slid it on the third finger of her right hand.

Mary Anne looked confused. "Aren't you supposed to wear it on your left hand?"

"Yes, but I'll wait until the war is over and Ray returns. Then *he* can put it on." Janet looked over at her mother. "You don't look very surprised."

"He wrote and asked my permission."

"What did you say?"

"I told him that you were almost twenty, and capable of making up your own mind."

"Thank you," she said, standing to give her mother a hug. "I guess I am old enough to decide, aren't I? These past two years have been full of letters . . . I guess Ray and I have both grown up a lot since we first met." Janet held out her hand so her sisters could admire the twinkling round diamond.

"He's a man now, just like Rob. When they went off to war they were kids, but not anymore." Martha's eyes filled with tears. "We'll just keeping praying that God brings them home safely."

HE NEVER EXPECTED her to be there at the train station. He hadn't told her when he'd be coming because he didn't know himself. The trains were packed these days, with servicemen and their families returning home now that the war had finally ended.

It had taken longer for the war to end in the Pacific, but Ray hadn't been there to hear the news anyway. In May he'd taken a bullet on Dakeshi Ridge while patching up a casualty and had become one himself. He was flown off Okinawa and eventually ended up in a hospital in San Diego. He didn't remember much of the trip.

Ray didn't wave and try to attract her attention right away. He just wanted to look at her for a moment, make sure the attractive, composed blonde was actually Janet Fridrich. *His* Janet Fridrich. He studied her profile as she studied the people lining up in the lunchroom for sandwiches and coffee. It was a blistering hot Saturday afternoon in September, but somehow Ray knew that the Nebraskans wouldn't let anyone continue their trip without something to eat.

Ray smiled. He didn't plan to continue East for a few more days, only until Janet agreed to go with him. Mr. and Mrs. Raymond Sandetti would return home together. He was a civilian now, and glad of it.

She looked pretty, her cheeks flushed, her golden hair wavy to the shoulders of her yellow print dress. She looked like the girl he'd spent the last two-and-a-half years dreaming about. And suddenly his feet refused to move forward, to bring him closer to her. Ray Sandetti, veteran of the invasions of Guadalcanal, New Britain and Okinawa, was suddenly scared to death. He recognized the feeling of fear—he'd experienced it often enough—but he'd never actually stood frozen before. Someone would yell, "Medic!" and he'd do his job, afraid or not. Now, he thought wryly, jamming his trembling hands into his civilian pants pockets, unless

Janet called for first aid, he could be in danger of being stuck here for hours.

Janet replaced the tray of sandwiches and met the amused gaze of a tall, brown-eyed man. At first she looked away, unwilling to encourage a stranger's attention. Then she looked back, wondering why he looked familiar. She couldn't believe it was Ray, though she'd met every train she could, without inconveniencing Doc. Ray stood there as casual as he could be, hands in his pockets and a secret smile on his face. No longer a homesick boy, but a self-assured man. A handsome one, though he was too thin. When he moved toward her she saw the power, the easy grace of a man who possessed the kind of strength that had enabled him to survive a war. She mouthed his name silently. "Ray?"

When he smiled and moved forcefully through the crowd, she knew it was him. But what would he think of her? He'd been halfway around the world—would he want an unsophisticated country girl after all this time?

Janet hurried around the table and met Ray as he slipped through the crowd toward her. He grinned, and grasped her shoulders, pulling her to him. His lips found hers, and she melted against him as he kissed her for a long, long moment. When he lifted his head, Janet opened her eyes and heard some of the people around them chuckling.

"Peaches," he murmured, "I've dreamed about that kiss."

"Me, too."

He wrapped her in his arms for a long, bone-shattering hug, until someone in the crowd yelled, "Take it outside, man! You're in the chow line!"

Ray chuckled and pulled Janet out of the building and into the bright sunshine. "Let me look at you," he said, holding her hands and stepping back. "Just as pretty as I remembered. Just as beautiful as your pictures."

She grinned back up at him. "So are you. Handsome, I mean, even without the uniform. You must have broken a lot of hearts these past years."

He shook his head. "Nah. I spent a lot of time writing letters, though. And dreaming about coming back here to see if you kept your promise." He lifted her right hand and saw the diamond shining back at him. "Good. It's right there where you said it would be." Ray looked down into those beautiful blue eyes. "Well, Peaches, are you going to marry me?"

"I think you'd better kiss me again before I decide," she murmured, standing on tiptoe to put her arms around his neck. "After all, this is only the second time we've met."

"Yes, ma'am." His lips met hers again in a more leisurely kiss; this time Ray knew he had all the time in the world. Neither one of them was going anywhere for a long, long while. Her mouth tasted sweet, her lips were warm and soft and willing. She pressed against him and he thought he would die from sheer pleasure. When he was afraid he would lose control, he broke off the kiss and smiled.

"If we don't stop now, we won't be able to." He kissed her forehead. "I'd planned a honeymoon in Colorado, up in the mountains. What do you say?"

Janet took a deep breath. "Tell me you don't have to get back on that train." He shook his head. "You can stay?"

"Yes. For a few days." *Until you can go with me.* She tugged at his hand. "Well, come on, then. You're coming home with me. That is, if you don't mind sleeping on the sun porch. We have two more boarders since I wrote last, so the house is pretty full."

"I don't mind at all, honey. Just give me a sec to get my gear."

"I'll go with you," she said, smiling up at him. "I don't want you out of my sight."

"Peaches," he said, kissing her once again before turning toward the station, "that's one thing you don't have to worry about."

"MARRY ME NOW," Ray demanded. "This week."

"I can't." She'd spent the best three days of her life with him. From the moment he'd stepped foot inside the house he'd become part of the family. Even Mama had perked up, happy to spoil a young man who reminded her so much of her son.

"Or won't."

"Ray," Janet pleaded, her heart breaking. "I can't leave my mother. She's been sick since Rob was killed, and that was nine months ago."

"Honey, I've waited a long time to get my life back. Four years." He swept his hand through his hair. "I've lost too much time. My parents need me, you know I have big plans for the market! I want to *be* somebody, Peaches." He frowned at her. "I want to be able to give you everything you deserve, but I don't want to be apart from you any longer, don't you see?"

Janet nodded, miserable as she sat next to him on the porch swing. He'd been restless since he arrived, always in motion, drinking coffee, pacing throughout the house as if he couldn't sit still. He was a man who wanted to get on with his life, and she didn't blame him; she just couldn't help him. "I don't either, but I have no choice. Since Robbie died, Mama has needed me so much."

"She has Mary Anne and Lou."

"And they're both still in school. I've been looking after them and running the house and cooking for the boarders, too."

He walked over to the window, his hands in his pockets. "I've already been here three days, honey, and my family is waiting for me. I told them I was bringing home my bride, you know."

"I know," she whispered. "I'm just asking you to wait a little longer."

He turned to her, but he wasn't smiling. "All right. A little longer." A glance down at her hands clasped in her lap caused his frown to deepen. He walked over, knelt in front of her and took her hands in his. He slipped the diamond off her right hand. "Will you marry me, Janet?" he asked, his face serious.

"Yes."

He held her left hand and slid the ring onto her finger, then kissed the back of her hand as he held it tightly. "Is that a promise?"

"It's a promise," she agreed, looking into his eyes and wishing she could memorize the love she saw there.

"Then I guess I'll have to be satisfied with that." He tried to smile, but couldn't manage it. "You'll come to me as soon as you can?"

Janet nodded, but the thought of leaving her family and the only home she'd ever known gave her an uneasy feeling, as if she was being torn in half. "As soon as I can."

"I'LL BE SEEING YOU, Peaches," he whispered against her hair, and then he was away from her, stepping onto the eastbound train. She didn't think she could bear saying goodbye at the station, but she managed to see him off without throwing herself at him one more time. So she waved, tears streaming down her face, until the train was out of sight and she was the only person left standing on the platform watching the empty tracks. After two-and-a-half years and 412 letters, Raymond Giovanni Sandetti had left her. And from the way her heart was breaking, she wondered if she would ever see him again.

3

"I THINK I've found a surefire method."

Sarah McGrath looked up from the stack of papers she was trying to correct and smiled at Betty, known as Mrs. Banks to the fourth-graders at McDonald Elementary.

"A surefire method for what? Grading papers?" She'd planned to finish the social studies tests before she headed home, but plowing through the colonization of early America was taking longer than she'd thought it would, especially in the crowded faculty room. Sarah usually didn't mind the noise; it was a welcome contrast to life at home.

"No. How to tell what a man is really like," Betty replied, taking a sip of her coffee as she sat down in the chair opposite Sarah's. "I discovered it this weekend."

Sarah put down the red pen and leaned forward. Betty was divorced, thirty-four, outspoken and incredibly popular with men. She was also a great teacher and Sarah's best friend. "Okay, tell me all about it. What did you do this past weekend that led to such a discovery?"

"Soccer," Betty said, her dark hair falling forward.

"If he plays soccer you know what he's really like? Or do you have to play soccer with him?"

"Quit fooling around and listen. All you have to do is stand beside a man at his child's soccer game and bingo!"

"Bingo—what?"

Betty grinned. "You listen to him. Does he mumble? Curse the coach? Yell at his daughter? Or does he remain calm, amused and keep the sport in perspective?"

"My guess is that your new man mumbled, cursed and yelled at his daughter."

Betty nodded. "Yep. He acted like a real idiot." She took another swallow of her coffee. "So much for thinking I'd met the man of my dreams."

"Well, at least you never give up trying. You're so optimistic."

"Not optimistic," her friend corrected. "Romantic. Don't you believe in love at first sight or fate or the kind of meeting that was meant to be?"

"Only in the movies."

"Don't you think love at first sight could happen, though? Like in *South Pacific* or *Casablanca*?"

"Not really. That some-enchanted-evening kind of love might make a good musical, but it's not practical for real life."

"There must be something wrong with you, Sarah," her friend declared. "You're not romantic at all."

"I come from a long line of practical midwesterners."

"You're only twenty-seven. There's still hope."

Sarah chuckled. "If you say so."

"How's the Christmas play coming along?"

Sarah grimaced. "It's going to be, uh, a real learning experience."

"For you or your class?"

"For everyone." Sarah pushed her glasses up on the bridge of her nose. "They've taken *A Christmas Carol* and rewritten it for the nineties."

"Sounds like a good creative exercise."

"Yes, but a little too creative. We started rehearsing this afternoon, after the lunch recess. I'm hoping one afternoon a week will do it, but I don't know. The kids are all wound up and it's not even Thanksgiving yet."

"I have to hand it to you, Sarah. You sure do throw yourself into the Christmas pageant each year. I don't know how you do it, but it's always fun to see what your kids come up with."

"Thanks." Sarah knew exactly why she did it each year, but no one save herself and her aunt would ever know. Christmas was always hard, and the busier she was, the better off she'd be. Sarah McGrath always looked forward to December 26th.

"Are you still having your football party?"

"Sure," Sarah answered, stacking her papers and sliding them into her oversize canvas tote. "It's a tradition, isn't it?"

"What do you want me to bring?"

"What would you like to?"

"How about the usual killer bean dip?"

"Great." Sarah stood and lifted her coat from the metal chair beside her. "I'm heading home before it gets dark."

"Want a ride?"

"No, thanks. I'll walk. I'm going to stop at the library and pick up something to read tonight. It's one of those nights when I just want to have a hot bath and get in bed with a good book."

"A romance, I hope?"

Sarah shook her head. "A mystery."

"ARE WE THERE yet?"

"It's the next exit," Nicholas Ciminero told his boss. He dropped the map of Nebraska, folded so North Platte and Highway 80 were easily visible on the neat rectangle, onto the seat of the car. The older man picked it up and kept it in his hand.

"It's hot in here," Ray said, pushing the button to roll down his window as Nicholas guided the rented Oldsmobile along Interstate 80.

"No, it's not," Nick answered, his voice mild. "It's November. It even looks like it could snow."

"Well, turn the heat down before I die. I don't want to die now," the old man muttered, closing the window.

"The heat's not on. You turned it off seventy miles ago and my foot is frozen to the gas pedal." Nick shot Ray a worried glance. It wasn't like Ray to complain. But Ray wasn't acting like himself at all. And hadn't since six weeks ago, when he'd agreed to make the trip to Denver to investigate the possibilities of expanding the business into the western states. Nick had been pushing that idea for almost two years, but he had a feeling that Ray wouldn't have finally agreed if there hadn't been something else on his mind. Although Nick had known Raymond Sandetti since he was ten years old, Nick also knew that Raymond was a very private man and that the only reason he'd been included on this trip, instead of staying in Colorado to take care of business, was to drive the car. Ray didn't mind short trips, but he flatly refused to drive farther than fifteen miles in any direction.

"How many miles?"

"A few," Nick replied. "Are you going to tell me why we're going to North Platte—a town in Nebraska I've never even heard of—instead of staying in Denver?"

"We saw everything there was to see in Denver. It was supposed to be a vacation, too, you know."

"We saw the U.S. Mint and the state capitol. There are probably a few things we missed." *Like touring about fifty grocery stores, and interviewing food brokers. If Ray was serious about expanding the business, that is.*

"We went up a mountain, didn't we?"

Nick grinned. "Usually the idea is to stay up on the mountain and learn to ski." When Ray didn't answer, Nick looked over at him once again.

Raymond Sandetti was a tall man, strongly built, with silver hair that framed a face that could once have been called handsome. He didn't smile often, but he was a smart man who could be trusted. A man who'd earned Nick's respect in the years they'd worked together.

Nick drove off the highway onto the exit ramp and then stopped at the main road. He turned to Ray and raised his eyebrows. "Now what? You're calling the shots."

"Left."

"Left," Nick repeated, and put on the blinker. He waited for two pickup trucks to go by, then turned onto the road. They passed gas stations, motels and something called Scout Ranch—which was a Buffalo Bill gift shop—before Ray spoke again.

"Just keep going straight."

Nick wished he was pulling the car into a motel parking lot. Better yet, into a restaurant parking lot. It was after three, but they'd had a late breakfast and Ray hadn't wanted to stop for lunch. "We're spending the night here, right?"

"Yes. Watch where you're going."

"You've memorized that map, haven't you?"

"I didn't have to," he replied. "Just drive, Nicholas. And take your time."

North Platte was a small town, with a mall and several fast-food restaurants. Neat houses lined the street, Nick noted as he slowed down to thirty miles an hour. "Do you know where you're going?"

"Of course I do. I'm not senile," Ray grumbled. "Take a left on Fourth Street."

Nick did as he was told, thoroughly mystified by his boss's behavior. Ray was only snappish when he was nervous, which meant the old man must be in pretty bad shape. As far as Nick knew, Raymond Sandetti had never been in Nebraska. He certainly didn't have business contacts there, so why was **he** so determined to spend a cloudy November afternoon in a town in the middle of the state?

"Ray..." Nick began, intending to get some answers once and for all.

"Slow down," the old man ordered. He adjusted his glasses and peered out the window. "It should be here somewhere."

"What?"

"Her house."

"Whose house?"

"Stop. *Stop.*"

Nick stepped on the brakes and pulled the car over to the curb. The old man's attention was focused upon a large two-story brick home. It was a beautiful house, obviously built in the late 1800s for a prosperous family. It had been well cared for over the years and sat, proud and graceful, on a large rectangle of lawn marked only by a curved brick driveway.

Nick started to question Ray again, but the intense look on the man's face stopped him. Something personal was going on here, something Nick realized he had no part of, maybe even no right to know anything about. He turned the engine off, put the car in Park, and waited. He wasn't a patient man, but he did know when to keep his mouth shut. Most of the time.

Five minutes went by. Nick zipped his heavy down parka and put on his leather gloves. Ray shivered, as if he had finally noticed the lack of heat. He shot his vice president an apologetic look. "Well . . ." he started.

Nick waited. "Are you going in?"

"Don't pull up in the driveway."

Nick looked around. Other cars were parked along the street. "All right. Is there someone you're looking for inside that house?"

Ray reached for the door handle. "I don't even know if she still lives there."

"She?"

Ray continued as if he hadn't heard Nick's question. "But someone inside that house might know what happened to the family who lived there." With a softly muttered oath he opened the door and strode across the lawn.

Nick grabbed the keys from the ignition, locked the doors, and hurried to catch up with his boss. He didn't know what was going on, but he sure wouldn't find out by freezing his tail off in the Achieva. He caught up with Ray as he rang the doorbell on the side of the large white door.

"See that?" Ray asked, pointing to the brass mail slot in the door.

"Yes, but what—"

The door opened to reveal a medium-size older woman. Nick guessed she would be in her early sixties. She wore gray slacks and a white fluffy sweater that highlighted her wavy silver hair. She looked like the kind of grandmother who read stories while children nestled in her lap. She glanced at both men, then said, "Yes? Can I help you?"

Long seconds ticked past as Nick waited for Raymond to say something. Finally Nick felt he had to speak before the woman slammed the door in their faces. "Excuse us, please. I think we're at the wrong house."

She smiled, her blue eyes crinkling at the corners. "Who are you looking for? Maybe I can help."

"Janet," Raymond whispered, steadying himself with one hand against the doorframe. "Janet Fridrich."

The woman's face drained of color and Nick wondered if he could reach her before she dropped to the polished wood floor. He started toward her but Ray's arm blocked his way. Ray's fingertips were as white as the painted wood he gripped.

"Ray?" she gasped.

"Yes, Peaches, it's me." He nodded. "Raymond Giovanni Sandetti. From Providence, Rhode Island."

Then, to Nick's surprise, the woman took two steps forward and hesitated, as if she wasn't sure what to do next. She reached up with one small veined hand and touched Ray's rigid cheek. "It can't be," she said softly. "Not after all these years."

Nick swallowed the lump in his throat. Obviously there was more to the story. Much more. He stepped back, feeling like an intruder, as his employer put his arms around Janet Fridrich and held on tightly. Long moments passed, until Nick shivered in the cold wind.

"I'm being rude," Janet sniffed, pulling away from Ray's embrace. "I'm making you stand out in the cold. Come in, come in." She stepped back to let the two men enter. "I can't believe this, Raymond."

Raymond started forward, then stopped.

"Ray?" Nick touched his back and saw his face was ashen. "Are you all right?"

"My medicine," he managed to say.

"Where?"

"Pocket."

"Here," Janet said, "you just lean on me and come into the living room." She shot Nick a questioning look before turning back to Ray. Nick grabbed his waist and guided him to one of two large cream sofas in a living room that ran the length of the house.

"Lean back," she said, sitting beside him.

Nick felt in Ray's coat pocket until he found a small vial of pills. He looked at the label. Nitroglycerin. He'd had no idea there was anything wrong with Ray's heart. Janet took the bottle from him, opened it and shook out a tiny pill which she placed under Ray's tongue.

Then she turned to Nick. "Let's get his coat off."

Nick hesitated. "I think I should take him to the hospital."

"No," Ray rasped. "No hospital. Feeling better."

Janet nodded her agreement. "You're getting some color back in your face."

Nick tried to protest. "But—"

Ray took Janet's small hand into his large one and held on tightly. "Still beautiful," he said.

"I should have recognized you right away," Janet admitted. "I just didn't believe my eyes."

"Janet," he began.

"Shh," she said. "Don't try to talk. We have plenty of time for that."

Ray nodded.

Janet turned to Nicholas. "You must be his son."

"No," Nick answered easily, well accustomed to the question. "I'm Ray's assistant, Nick Ciminero."

"Like a son," Ray interjected, struggling to sit up. He frowned as Nick started toward him with a restraining hand. "Stop looking like that. I'm much better."

"Let's get you to a doctor," Nick said. "Now."

Ray shook his head. "No. I know what I'm doing."

Nick backed away, but he didn't like Ray's refusal. "I sure as hell hope you do."

Janet helped Ray take off his coat. "You're still as stubborn as ever, I see."

"I never did change much, I suppose." His eyes grew sad. "I should have."

"Why are you here, Ray?"

Again Nick felt that he was intruding on something so private he felt like an eavesdropper. He slowly backed away from the couch and then stood awkwardly in the doorway of the living room.

"To see you," Ray replied. "To see what happened to you. Are you married?"

"Widowed," she said. "For the past six years."

"I'm sorry."

"So am I."

Nick realized Ray was feeling better, or otherwise he wouldn't be able to carry on a conversation. But he would corner him later, find out how long Ray had been carrying a vial of nitroglycerin tablets. He glanced around the foyer. A carved oak staircase rose behind him, and off to one side was a dining room. Shades of yellow and white dominated the interior of the house, a warm contrast to the gray winter afternoon.

Nick turned as the front door opened and a young woman entered. Her cheeks were flushed from the cold, although her long emerald coat covered most of her. Silky chestnut hair swept over her shoulders as she turned to stare at Nick.

"Who—"

"Shh," he cautioned, putting his finger to his lips. "There's some kind of reunion going on in the living room."

She put down a bulging canvas bag, pulled off her gloves and stepped to the entrance of the living room. Then she turned back to Nick. "Who is that man and who are you?"

"Who are *you?*" He almost smiled at the suspicious expression on her face, but he caught himself in time.

"I live here."

"Janet's daughter?"

"Niece. How do you know Janet? And who is that man with my aunt?"

"Ray Sandetti, my employer. I'm not sure what's going on either, but I think they knew each other many years ago. He called her 'Peaches' and she hugged him. Right now they're catching up."

Janet's niece once again peered into the living room then turned back to Nick. "I'm afraid I don't understand."

"Neither do I," Nicholas replied. "But maybe we could figure it out together. All I know is that my boss insisted on coming to this house. After he did, he had chest pains and ended up on your aunt's couch, popping nitroglycerin."

Concern flooded the young woman's eyes. "Is he all right now? I could call a doctor."

"He won't let me." Nick ran his hand through his hair and suddenly realized how tired he was. "Do you have any instant coffee? I've been on the road for hours."

She hesitated for a moment. "All right. Follow me," she said, leading the way through the dining room and past swinging doors to an enormous kitchen. "But I hate instant. I'll make a fresh pot of coffee while you tell me exactly who you are and what is going on."

Nick shrugged off his coat and draped it over the back of a Windsor chair. He leaned against the wide white island and watched the woman fill a glass carafe with water and prepare the coffeepot. When she had switched on the pot, she unbuttoned her emerald coat and unwound the bright scarf from her neck. Then she tossed them over one of the counter stools and sat down on the empty one.

"I'm Nicholas Ciminero. From Rhode Island."

"The smallest state in the union?"

"That's right."

"Well, Mr. Ciminero, if you're here for the night, I'm afraid we don't take in guests in the fall or winter," she said. "Janet can't handle the work alone."

"Call me Nick. And we're not guests," he said. "Is this a boarding house?"

"My aunt has had a bed-and-breakfast inn here for years, until the doctor told her she had to slow down. I'm a teacher, so I'm able to help her in the summer. But once school starts, she's supposed to relax and concentrate on her volunteer work. Doctor's orders."

"We're not guests," he repeated. "Just brief visitors." And he looked at the beautiful woman with the hazel eyes and silky hair and wondered why he felt regret at the thought of never seeing her again. "And you still haven't told me your name."

Her lips, a vestige of peach lipstick remaining, curved into a smile. "Sarah. Sarah McGrath."

"What do you teach?"

"Fifth grade." She slipped off the stool and pulled a tray from one of the cabinets.

She didn't look like any teacher he'd ever had. He watched as she tucked a strand of hair behind her ear, revealing a gold hoop. He noticed she wasn't wearing a ring. She looked about twenty-three, but for some strange reason he hoped she was older. He was thirty-five, heading toward forty at an alarming speed. Nick didn't know why he cared about Sarah McGrath's age, but he hoped she wasn't fresh out of college.

"Do you take milk or sugar?"

"Both, thanks."

Sarah took a quart of milk from the refrigerator and poured some into a small pitcher, then placed it on the tray beside the coffee cups. Silver spoons, a sugar bowl and paper napkins completed the tray.

She lifted it and headed toward the door. "I don't know about you, but I think we need to find out what's going on in there."

Nick agreed and slid off the stool. "I'll carry the coffeepot."

Janet sat beside Ray on the cream print sofa, and they were talking softly when the young couple entered the room. Janet looked up and smiled at her niece. "Sarah! I didn't hear you come in." She held out her hand as Sarah set the tray on the coffee table. "Come meet an old friend of mine, Ray Sandetti. Ray, this is my dear niece, Sarah."

Sarah held out her own hand as the older man took it in a surprisingly firm grasp. "Hello," she said.

"It's a pleasure," he murmured, glancing between the two women. "There's certainly a family resemblance."

"Sarah is Louella's child," Janet supplied.

"Your youngest sister?"

Janet nodded.

"And how is the rest of your family?"

"Mary Anne is in Omaha. Her family's all grown now. And Louella, Sarah's mother, died twelve years ago this month."

"I'm sorry," he said, his glance including them both. "Your friend—"

"Nick," he supplied, sitting down on the sofa opposite his employer, leaving room for Sarah to sit beside him. He watched as she hesitated, then sat down, leaving at least two feet of upholstered fabric between them as she leaned forward over the tray.

"Nick said you weren't feeling very well. Would you like some coffee or would you rather have tea? The tea is decaffeinated."

"Coffee will be fine, thank you." Ray ignored the question about his health. "I'm sorry you have to go to all this trouble."

He didn't look sorry, Nick decided. Ray looked very pleased with himself. He was obviously content to let two women wait on him, if that's what they wanted to do. Nick was no closer to learning what Ray was up to, except that Ray had wanted to see Janet, obviously a woman he hadn't been able to forget. And the shock of seeing her had sent his heart racing.

"Thanks." Nick took the cup of coffee Sarah handed him. "It's been a long day."

Janet smiled at him. "I understand you've been to Denver on business. How wonderful that you and Ray took the time to stop in North Platte."

Took the time? It was the entire reason for this so-called "vacation." Nick was catching on that the trip to Denver was Ray's cover for the Nebraska side trip. "Ray insisted," Nick said, taking a quick sip of the coffee. "I don't think he would have had it any other way."

Ray raised a warning eyebrow, telling Nick he was close to going too far with his teasing. Nick was relieved to see that Ray's color was better and he looked almost back to normal. As soon as they finished this visit with the ladies, he'd take Ray to the nearest hospital. He'd seen *H* signs on the way in, so there must be some sort of medical facility that could check out Ray's heart. Nick didn't intend to leave North Platte until he'd learned that Ray was okay to travel back to Denver. Their work there could wait, and so could their vacation. At the worst, Nick could fly back to Denver on his own next month. The most important thing was to get Ray to a doctor and find out what was going on with his heart.

"Would you like some more?"

Nick looked down at his empty cup, unaware he'd finished the coffee. He held it out to Sarah once again. "Please. Then we'd better get on our way."

Ray frowned. Janet looked surprised. "Oh, no, Ray. So soon?"

"Well," he hesitated.

"Where are you going next?"

"We're just driving," Ray managed. "We've taken a working vacation, but accomplished most of the work in Denver last week."

"Then you haven't made any plans?"

Nick almost groaned out loud. He knew what was coming, and from the hopeful expression on Ray's face, the old man did, too.

"Not really," Ray fibbed.

"Then don't rush off, not when we've so much to catch up on."

"Aunt Janet," Sarah began, clearly ready to bid the guests farewell. "I'm sure they're very busy men."

But Ray shook his head. "We're on vacation."

"And you must have needed one, too," Janet said. "You shouldn't rush off. Maybe you need to stay in one place for a few days instead of getting back into a car."

"Well, then," Ray murmured. "Maybe we'll stick around for a while longer." He looked over at Nick, as if he'd finally remembered who Nick was. "We have reservations at the Holiday Inn just outside of town, don't we?"

Nick looked at his watch. "Yes, and it's about time we checked in." He turned to Janet. "Is there a hospital in town? I think Ray should see a doctor."

"No." Ray put his cup on the tray and reached for his coat.

"Why not?"

"I don't need to, that's why." He looked to Janet and smiled. "I'm getting better every minute."

She smiled back, and once again Nick felt the uncomfortable feeling that he was trespassing into private territory. He looked over at Sarah and saw an expression that echoed the same feeling on her face.

"I think we should cut this vacation short and head back home," Nick said. "If you won't go to a doctor here, then at least check in with your doctor in Providence."

"I have a better idea," Janet said. "A compromise." Three pairs of eyes turned her way, but only Ray looked as if he was going to like what she had to say. "Stay here," she said. "I hate the thought of your staying in a hotel when I have plenty of room here at the house. You can stay as long as you want. Rest. Have a home-cooked meal. See how you feel in the morning." She placed her hand over his. "Please? We have plenty of room, don't we, Sarah?"

Sarah didn't answer, but Janet didn't appear to notice.

"We can't—" Nick started to protest, but a hard look from Ray stopped him. Ray wanted to be here, with this woman, in this house. Nick knew better than to say another word. Raymond Sandetti's mind was made up. And when that happened, nothing in the world would change it.

4

SARAH FOLLOWED her aunt upstairs to the second floor and watched as she opened the linen cupboard. "Aunt Janet, what do you think you're doing?"

The silver-haired woman rifled through the stack of sheets. "Finding appropriate linen. I'll need a twin set for Ray and a queen for the room upstairs."

"Let me do that," Sarah said, reaching into the cupboard. "Don't try to act innocent. You know what I mean. You're not supposed to run the business in the wintertime. It's too much for you."

"How could it be too much having two men in the house? And I'm not running the business. They're guests."

"Guests." Sarah shook her head. "Couldn't they simply have dinner with us and sleep in a hotel?"

"No."

Sarah found the sheets and pulled them off the shelf. "I'll make up the beds. But how long do you think they're going to stay?"

Janet smiled to herself, then at her niece. "Until they decide to leave, dear. As long as Ray wants."

Sarah couldn't ignore the look of happiness in her aunt's eyes. "Who is Ray Sandetti, Aunt Janet? Was he someone very special?"

"He was a friend," she replied. "Is that so hard to understand?"

"No," Sarah said, giving up the argument for now. "You've been taking in strays for years, and you started with me. I guess there isn't anything I can say to change your mind about this. I'll try to help as much as I can."

"Don't worry about a thing, dear." She patted Sarah's cheek. "You weren't a 'stray.' You were—are—my family. And don't worry. Ray and I have a lot of catching up to do. Besides, how much trouble can two men cause?"

"I DON'T THINK this is a good idea," Nick said. He looked around the small room tucked behind the ground-floor staircase and watched as Ray unpacked his small suitcase.

"I know. You've said that a few times, Niccolo."

"And you refuse to listen."

The old man shrugged. "I promised I'd see a doctor if I had any more trouble with my heart, didn't I?"

"Yes, but—"

"And I said I'd make this a business arrangement with Janet, didn't I?"

"Yes, but—"

"It's a perfect situation. You can't argue with that. I'm staying on this floor so I don't have to climb the stairs and you have a private room on the third floor."

"Ray—"

"You should have no problems with this, Nick. You got your trip to Denver, and now we're taking some extra time here in Nebraska."

"But work—"

"Can wait," Ray stated, zipping his empty suitcase as if he planned never to use it again. "After almost fifty years it can damn well wait."

Nick shoved his hands in his pockets. "This isn't like you, Ray. Maybe it's the medication."

"No," the man said. "Maybe it's looking at my life and wondering what I could have done, and what I *should* have done differently."

"We all do that, Ray."

"Tell me that when you're alone and looking at seventy candles on the birthday cake." He grinned, his dark eyes twinkling. "I won't be here, of course, but some young man of thirty-five will be standing next to you and won't understand a word you have to say and all of a sudden you'll remember this conversation."

"Ray—"

"Unless, of course, you learn from this."

"Whatever *this* is," Nick muttered. "*This* is a mystery."

Ray patted him on the shoulder. "No. The mystery is why she let me stay."

"I see," Nick said after a long moment. "You broke her heart and you never forgot her."

Ray shook his head. "I wish it was that simple."

"What are we doing here, Ray?"

The older man ignored the question and put his hand on Nick's shoulder. "Promise me, Niccolo. Promise me you will not interfere, that you will help me."

Nick would die for him, and—damn him—the old man knew it. "How?"

"Time," he answered. "Just give me a little more time with her."

"That's simple enough," he agreed, and Ray squeezed his shoulder. "But what about your health? Your heart—"

"Has belonged to Janet since 1942 and broke a long time ago. The rest doesn't matter."

"You're a stubborn old goat."

"Don't worry so much, Nick. I've decided I'm going to live a long time."

"I'M TAKING YOU out to dinner."

"Nonsense. Everything's all made."

"Please, Jan."

"No." Janet handed Ray four place mats. "You can set the table. If you feel up to it."

"Why wouldn't I feel up to it?" he grumbled. "I feel well enough to take you out to a nice meal, that's how I feel."

Janet ignored his grumbling and opened the oven door to check the roast. "It's cold outside and warm in here. Why go out?"

"So you can be waited on," Ray said, dropping the place mats on the wide trestle table.

"I don't need to be waited on."

Sarah entered the kitchen, having changed into corduroy slacks and a dark green sweater. "If you can stop her from working, Mr. Sandetti, it would be a miracle."

"Please, call me Ray."

Nick opened the kitchen door and stepped into the warm room. "Something smells good in here."

"Pot roast," Janet supplied. "And it's ready. All I have to do is warm up the rolls."

"Warm them up tomorrow night," Ray said. "And let us take you out to dinner."

"No."

Nick turned to Sarah and raised his eyebrows. Sarah shrugged her shoulders, but didn't say anything. Obviously he didn't know what was going on any more than she did. Ray and Janet were on their own with this discussion. Sarah liked the idea that Nick didn't know what was going on either. She'd hate being the only one.

Ray frowned. "Tomorrow then."

"Tomorrow would be lovely."

Ray's expression brightened. "You're a difficult woman, Janet."

"Not any more difficult than you are," she replied. She took four plates from the cupboard. "Here. Finish your job. Nick and Sarah, you can sit down at the table."

Sarah realized she'd have to continue to keep an eye on Janet. She would work herself half to death spoiling her houseguests and not taking care of herself. Any minute now she'd start baking dessert and planning a four-course breakfast. Sarah knew that the minute she left for school, Janet would make work for herself. She was never happier than when she was doing something for someone else.

"There's no use arguing," Sarah told the two men. "You won't win."

Ray shook his head. "Don't I know it," he grumbled, taking the plates to the table. Sarah took them from him and put them on the four checked place mats while Janet carried a platter of pot roast and placed it in the center of the table.

"Sit down, please," she said. "I'm just going to get the potatoes."

"All of this was for the two of you?"

"I find it hard to cook for two," she admitted. "We would have eaten this for several nights."

It did look like a feast. Sarah noticed her aunt had put out her best strawberry jam, bread-and-butter pickles and a loaf of whole wheat bread. She'd used the Blue

Willow platter for the meat, a sure sign that this dinner was special. "It looks wonderful, Aunt Janet."

"Thank you, dear," she said, taking her seat at the head of the table. "Now," she said, "everyone help themselves."

Sarah, seated across the table from Nick, decided she would find out more about Janet's guests. Someone had to do it, and it looked like she was the only one. "What brings you to North Platte, Nick?"

"We've actually been in Denver," Nick replied. "I'm trying to talk Ray into expanding his business into the Midwest and west."

Janet leaned forward. "What business, Ray?"

"Sandetti Specialties. We market Italian food products to grocery stores and small gourmet shops."

Sarah thought that was interesting. It wasn't what she expected. She'd assumed they'd come for the pheasant hunting. "Is there a market for that out here?"

Nick answered. "I'd like to think so."

Ray grinned. "Nick is trying to convince me. You young people think the world is such a small place."

"There's plenty of room out here for our products." Nick passed her the bowl of potatoes. "What do you think?"

"I wouldn't know about that. I'm not much of a cook," Sarah admitted.

"No?" Nick's eyebrows raised.

"No." Sarah wished he wasn't quite so handsome, that his dark brown eyes weren't quite so expressive or his gaze so attentive. She wasn't comfortable being so . . . studied. "What are you planning to do here in North Platte? Are you going on to Omaha and Des Moines?"

Ray shook his head. "I've seen enough, I think. I'll give it some thought, though."

"We need to return to Denver," Nick said.

"No," his boss countered. "We are now on vacation, Nicholas."

Sarah wanted to smile. Nobody she knew went to North Platte for a vacation.

"We were going skiing, too, remember?"

"You must see the canteen museum while you're here," Janet said. "It's closed in the winter, but I'll find someone who will open it for you. They tore down the original station years ago, but the museum has a lot of things you'll recognize."

"I'd like that," Ray agreed.

"Good. I'll call in the morning and see what I can do," she said.

"Will you go with me?"

Janet looked away and shook her head. "I don't think so."

"Why not?"

She just shook her head. "Would anyone like another roll?"

Nick asked a question about the house, and the conversation moved into that direction. Sarah knew her aunt was grateful for the change in topic. After dinner Sarah offered to clean up the kitchen. She hoped the rest of them would relax in the living room and she would enjoy the moments of privacy in the kitchen.

"I'll dry," Nick offered, carrying a stack of dirty plates to the counter. "Unless you'd rather I washed."

"We have a dishwasher, but thanks anyway."

"Then I'll clear the table."

"Thanks, but—"

"Good idea," Ray said, rising to his feet. "I'll help, too."

"No," Nick said. "You need to get some rest."

Janet patted his arm. "Come on, Ray. Let the young people have their way."

When they'd left, Sarah turned to Nick, who leaned over the table. "I really don't need any help."

He ignored her comment. "Where are the coffee cups?"

"Right there above your head."

He put the glasses on the counter, found a cup, then poured the remaining coffee into it and stuck it in the microwave. He drummed his fingers on the counter while he waited for it to heat up. Sarah turned on the faucet and began rinsing dishes.

"They want to be alone," he said.

"They do?"

He opened the door of the microwave, took a cautious sip of coffee and then leaned against the counter and looked at her. "Of course. Haven't you noticed?"

"Noticed what?"

"The way they look at each other."

"I think you're wrong."

"No, you don't. Not really. You just don't want to see what's going on."

She opened the dishwasher and started putting the dishes inside. "I know that for some mysterious reason we have two men staying in the house, two men I've never seen before." She looked back at him and smiled. "I'm sure you're both very nice people, but—"

"Aren't you used to having company?"

"In the summer, yes, but they're the same people who come back year after year. We don't get too many strangers."

"I see. Well, Ray isn't exactly a stranger."

"I've realized that."

"So, are we going to leave them alone?"

"I don't know. Let me be honest here, Nick. My aunt isn't in the best of health. She needs her rest, a lot of rest. And I can't help her now because I'm in school all day. I'm afraid that this will just be too much for her."

"All right. I can understand that. I'm not exactly thrilled that Ray is staying here, especially after the little episode with the nitroglycerin tablets this afternoon. I'd be happier if we were back in Rhode Island. But there isn't much I can do to change his mind. He's determined to see your aunt. I didn't know that when we drove into town, but I caught on pretty fast."

"She's the reason he came here?"

"Yes, I think so. And he's not going to leave until he's done whatever he's had on his mind from the beginning."

"Which could take days," she added, not happy with the realization.

"Not if we give them time together," Nick suggested, his dark eyes twinkling. "They obviously have some kind of past," he said, looking down at her. "Something from a long time ago, something we know nothing about. Look, Sarah, I'm anxious to get Ray back home, and you're worried about your aunt. So let's stay in this kitchen a very long time. Tell me the story of your life, wash the kitchen floor, anything." He grinned. "Let's give them time to talk privately. Then we can all go on with our lives."

Sarah had to admire the man's thinking. She found herself smiling back, despite her misgivings. He made sense, Nicholas Ciminero did. "You think you're pretty smart, don't you?"

He nodded. "Yeah."

"If this works, I might agree with you," she said. "Here," she said, handing him a soapy sponge. "You can wipe the counters."

"All right."

Sarah cleared her throat, ready to give him the abbreviated, G-rated version she gave to everyone else. "I was born west of town," she began, "on July 28, 1966."

"I SHOULDN'T HAVE let you talk me into this," Janet said, hesitating in the doorway of the museum. Ray took her arm and nudged her forward. "I work here all the time, and yet today I just don't think I can—"

"There's nothing that can hurt us now, Janet," he said.

"That's where you're wrong."

"No. These are good memories."

"Some of them are, some of them aren't. So many people come here to remember," she said, following him past the gift shop area into the museum section. "Even though the original building was torn down in the middle of the night by the railroad."

"That's a shame," he muttered, wandering through the exhibits. "I don't remember the piano," he said, stopping in front of a photograph of sailors gathered around the piano singing.

"We sat near it."

"I remember that meal." He smiled at her, and she didn't see a man close to seventy. She saw a young, handsome sailor with homesick eyes. "You asked if I wanted milk or coffee."

"You asked for my address instead."

He smiled. "You gave it to me."

"Not right away."

"No," he agreed. "Not right away."

They were silent, strolling through the room. Janet watched him examine the journals and read some of the entries in them. It would take hours, maybe days, to read them all. She wondered if he wanted to come back another time, and knew he would have to come by himself. She could not do this again. Even now, after only a few minutes, she wanted to open her purse and pull out a handkerchief and weep for a long, long while. And she didn't even know why, only knew the tears were filling her eyes and ready to overflow.

She was a sentimental old woman, that's what she was. And she had no business being here with the man she once loved, even if it had been over fifty years since she'd first set eyes on him. What was fifty years—the blink of an eye, perhaps? Time went by so fast. She'd put on a few pounds, turned gray, and her unreliable heart skipped a beat every once in a while. But standing here with Ray could take her back fifty years in the blink of an eye.

Janet forced herself to stand very still, to watch him peruse the journals and study the photographs on the wall. This was why he had come to North Platte, after all. She would give him the time he needed. Then he and that handsome young man who worked for him would drive back to Denver and expand the business of Italian food and a sentimental old woman would always remember a young man named Ray.

THE REHEARSAL for *A Christmas Carol* was not going well. Jimmy Dorset couldn't remember his lines and burped throughout the scene with Tiny Tim. Tiny Tim had fallen on the floor laughing. The girls in the class had rolled their eyes and turned to Miss McGrath for help.

Miss McGrath had been happy to hear the dismissal bell.

Now, longing for the quiet of her home, Sarah decided to go in the side kitchen door. With luck, the houseguests would be occupied elsewhere and she could sit at the table and make herself a cup of tea and decide what she could do to turn around the Christmas pageant. Or what punishment she could give Jimmy Dorset if he disrupted rehearsal again.

The smell of tomato sauce and garlic filled the entry, and Sarah passed the laundry area and went up three steps to the huge kitchen. Rock 'n' roll played from the radio and Nick, a dishcloth tied around his slim waist, stood at the stove stirring something in a large pot. He looked up and smiled when he saw her.

"Hello," he said cheerfully, leaving the spoon in the pot. "You're just in time."

"For what?"

"I just opened a bottle of wine." He lifted the bottle and poured a large portion into an empty wineglass. "I hate to drink alone."

Sarah took the offered glass and set it down on the island. "Thanks. You've been busy." She took off her coat and scarf, and put them on the window seat. "What are you doing?"

"Making dinner."

"How did you get that job?" She slid onto a stool and picked up the wineglass.

He lifted his own glass in a toast. "To 1942," he said, ignoring her question.

Sarah touched her glass with his and said, "Why? Is the wine that old?"

"I'm putting the puzzle together," he said. "Nineteen forty-two is when Janet and Ray met."

Interesting. "Where are they now?"

"They're both lying down. I ordered them to."

That didn't surprise Sarah. A nap on a cloudy November afternoon sounded pretty damn good right about now. Drinking wine with a handsome man who was also cooking dinner wasn't half bad either. She took another sip. "Nice wine. What is it?"

"You are a woman full of questions, aren't you?"

"Aren't you used to women who ask questions?"

He grinned. "There you go again. You told me you're concerned about Janet's health. I thought I could do something to help. I'm making dinner because that's what I do for a living, and I'd go crazy just sitting around this house with nothing to do. So I went shopping."

"I thought you were a businessman."

"I specialize in Italian food. I buy it, cook it and eat it."

Sarah thought of the *Christmas Carol* rehearsal and envied Nick's occupation. She sipped more of the rich red wine. "That doesn't sound like a hard job."

"It has its moments."

"What did they do today?"

"I'm not sure, but I know they went to the Buffalo Bill museum to see the canteen."

"Did Ray talk Aunt Janet into going with him?"

"He sure did. I watched as he turned on the charm and had her driving off with him in the car in no time at all. I stayed here and twiddled my thumbs until I decided to explore your town."

"There's not much to explore."

"I found what I needed, at least what I could make do with for dinner tonight." He reached over and re-filled her glass. "Drink up. There's plenty more in the car."

"The car?"

"I bought quite a few bottles in Denver. Some are my favorites, others I wanted to try."

"I like this one."

He drained his glass. "Yes. It's a dependable red."

"We can't just sit here and drink an entire bottle of wine. I'll fall off the stool if I drink much more."

"You're right. We need something to go with it."

He opened the refrigerator and pulled out a chunk of cheese. "A few crackers and cheese will do just fine."

Sarah watched as Nick arranged the cheese and crackers on a wooden cutting board. She felt warm and relaxed, and knew the wine was working. Maybe working a little too well. Still, it wasn't an unpleasant feeling. She needed to get out more. First thing tomorrow morning she'd talk to Betty about fixing her up with a date.

For now, she'd eat a few crackers and find out a little more about Nick Ciminero.

"So, what's for dinner?"

"Meatballs and spaghetti."

"You made meatballs?"

"Of course. Tomorrow we'll have lasagna."

"Tomorrow?"

"I hate to ruin your day, but I think we'll still be here tomorrow night."

"Why?"

"Ray is making plans for the weekend. Plans in North Platte."

"I think I'll take some more of that wine, please." She held out her glass. "A woman could get used to this," she said, watching him pour her another glass. "A man cooking dinner, serving hors d'oeuvres...."

"Obviously no one spoils you," he noted, topping off his own glass and tossing the empty bottle into the trash. "Have you ever been married?"

"No."

"Not even close?"

Sarah considered the question. "Close," she finally replied. "A very long time ago."

"What happened?"

"He changed his mind."

Nick lifted his glass and touched Sarah's. "To fools," he said.

"Him or me?"

"Him, of course."

"All right," she agreed, accepting the toast. "I'll drink to that. Besides, I've had a long day."

"Tell me."

"My class is doing their own version of *A Christmas Carol*. Scrooge entertained the rest of the cast by belching out his lines. Tiny Tim egged him on, and no one remembered their parts. This is supposed to be our contribution to the Christmas program."

"You are a very brave woman."

"I know," she agreed solemnly.

Nick pushed the cheese toward her. "You'd better eat something. You're getting morbid."

"Okay. This is very civilized."

"Well, I do my best."

"Your sauce is bubbling."

"It's supposed to," he said, but turned back to the stove to stir it again. "A slow bubble."

"How did you learn to cook like this? From your mother?"

He didn't turn around right away. "No. A woman I lived with."

"Oh." Sarah realized the wine had definitely gone to her head. He probably had many women in his life, maybe even lived with one right now. He certainly didn't act married, didn't act like he had to call anyone and say, "I'm in Nebraska and don't know when I'll be home."

He turned then and picked up his wineglass.

"You must love your work."

"I do." He grinned. "If Ray decides to stay here much longer, I'll have to find something to do besides cook. I'm not used to having this much time off." He scooped out a meatball and put it on a plate. "Here. Try it and see what a real Italian meatball tastes like."

"Can't you just go back to Rhode Island?"

"Not yet, not until I'm sure it's safe to leave Ray. He never told me he had heart trouble, and I don't like to leave him alone right now."

Sarah picked up the fork he handed her and took a bite of the meatball. It was heaven, tender and spicy in a rich tomato sauce. "It's incredible. If you're still here on Saturday you can make meatballs for the football party."

"All right. What team?"

She couldn't believe he'd asked that. "What *team?*"

"Yeah."

"Nebraska. It's the Nebraska-Oklahoma game."

"I don't know much about football."

"Then you're in the wrong state, Nick. College football is everyone's obsession."

"Tell you what, you teach me about Nebraska football and I'll teach you to make meatballs."

She laughed. "You don't know what kind of cook I am!"

"I'll risk it," he said.

"You're on," she agreed. "How soon is dinner?"

"Another hour, I think. Five-thirty okay?"

"It will give me time to sober up."

"You haven't had that much wine."

"Are you kidding? This is more than I'd drink in a month. You're a bad influence on me."

"Good."

"Good?"

"Of course." He shot her a wicked look. "That's another one of my specialties."

5

"LET ME GET THIS straight." Betty leaned forward across the lunch table. "Your aunt met a man she knew when she was young and then she invited him to stay at the house?"

"That's right."

"But it's so romantic."

"Not exactly." Sarah unwrapped her meatball sandwich and eyed it without much enthusiasm. "I can think of other ways to describe it."

"Such as?"

"Inconvenient. Strange."

"What's strange about it?"

"Well, these two men showed up on the front step and—"

"*Two* men?"

"Wait, I'm getting to that. The older one, Ray, is Aunt Janet's age and has a bad heart, and yet he wanted to come to North Platte to see her."

"Come from where?"

"That's the weird part. From Rhode Island, for heaven's sake."

"Was she happy to see him?"

"Yes. Really happy." Sarah put the sandwich down and picked up her coffee cup. "She insisted they stay as long as they want, and she and Ray have been together for the past two days."

Betty grinned. "There's more, isn't there?"

"The other one is younger, mid-thirties, very good-looking. And he cooks."

"He cooks?"

"Meatballs, lasagna. If it has tomato sauce on it, then Nick knows how to make it. He's bored to death, so he says, and when I told him I worried about Janet's health, he took over the cooking."

"What is he—a chef?"

"Sort of. He works for Ray Sandetti, the man Aunt Janet knows."

"Is he married?"

"No."

Betty leaned back in her chair. "This gets more interesting by the minute. What's the matter?"

"I don't know. He's too gorgeous, too charming, too . . . everything. He makes me nervous." *And he makes me think of bedrooms and how long it's been since anyone held me.*

"Now you really have me intrigued. A man has finally made Sarah McGrath nervous? A miracle. I can't wait to meet him. He will be at the football party, won't he?"

Sarah nodded. "Of course. He's making the meatballs."

"I'm impressed."

She almost smiled. Betty had quite a surprise in store for her. "Wait till you meet him."

"DON'T YOU HAVE anything red you can wear?"

Nick looked down at his soft denim shirt and back to Sarah, who looked about seventeen in her faded gray sweatshirt with a red University of Nebraska emblem on the front. A red turtleneck peeked above the round collar. "Why?"

"It's a tradition for my football parties."

He looked down into those gorgeous hazel eyes and forgot anything he ever knew about football. He could think of a few more enjoyable things to do with Sarah besides watch television. None of them required a crowd. Or food. Or wearing sweatshirts. "I *have* to wear red?"

Sarah nodded. "Or something with 'Nebraska' on it. Anything that shows your football spirit. I'll let you borrow a sweatshirt." She turned around and went back upstairs.

"You really don't have to go to all that trouble," he called, watching her cute little backside disappear around the landing. He liked it when she wore jeans. Since the day before yesterday he'd discovered himself watching Sarah McGrath and liking what he saw.

She wasn't thrilled with their company, he knew that, but some of her tension had eased when she'd realized that Janet wasn't overdoing it by entertaining her guests. And she'd liked his cooking. At least that was something. Since they were thrown together, they might as well make the most of an awkward situation and behave like two adults. The male adult would certainly like to get to know the female adult a whole lot better.

Sarah hurried back down the stairs and tossed Nick a red sweatshirt. "It's an extralarge."

"I really prefer my own clothes." Nick held up the sweatshirt and examined the yellow-haired farmer above the letters imprinted on the front of the shirt. "What's a cornhusker? I don't think this is my—"

"It's perfect. All you have to say is, 'Go Big Red!'"

"Go Big Red."

"With feeling," she added, smiling up at him before turning into the living room.

"Give me some time," he muttered, following her. "This midwestern enthusiasm is something I have to work up to."

Janet and Ray sat on one of the couches, sharing sections of the newspaper. They both looked up and smiled when Sarah and Nick entered the room.

"You'd better put that on, son," Ray said, proudly displaying his own new red sweatshirt. "It's tradition."

"So I see. We look like a platter of boiled lobsters." He tugged the shirt over his head.

Janet put down the paper and smiled. "You look very nice, Nick. And you've been a dear to make all that food."

"I've enjoyed having something to do." He glanced at Ray, hoping he got the message.

The old man picked up the paper again. "You've got to learn how to relax, Niccolo. You're on vacation, remember?"

No, he didn't remember. He thought he'd finally talked a stubborn old man into exploring new territory for Sandetti Specialties to conquer. He'd thought he'd see mountains and maybe learn to ski. He didn't know he'd be cooking for strangers in Nebraska and forced to wear someone else's clothes.

Sarah turned on the television set. Adjusting the color, she asked him, "What do you think?"

He thought he'd like to take her upstairs to that private third-floor bedroom and make love to her for three or four days. Unfortunately he was supposed to watch college football instead. "It's fine," he managed.

The doorbell rang and Sarah started to get up off the floor. Nick reached down to take her hand and pulled her to her feet.

"Come on," she said, tugging him toward the foyer. "You have to meet some other Nebraska fans."

He met Sarah's teaching friend Betty Banks and her son, Billie. And an older couple who lived next door, Jim and Ellen Johnson. Then Mark Price, the young music teacher who had recently graduated from the university, arrived with a bearded, blue-eyed giant called "Fin" who taught physical education in Sarah's school and enveloped her in a bear hug when she greeted him at the door. Nick couldn't believe that guy was Sarah's type, although Fin seemed likable enough when Nick shook his hand. He'd keep an eye on him, though. It never hurt to analyze the competition.

SARAH DIDN'T KNOW how Nick managed to sit beside her on the couch, but he did, his warm thigh touching hers in a distracting way. She leaned forward for another cracker, hoping to break the contact.

"The place is going crazy," Nick said, obviously surprised at the fans' behavior in the bleachers.

Sarah turned back to the television screen. The red-dressed crowd was going wild, cheering and jumping up and down. "We sacked their quarterback and that was their last down. They'll have to punt and it will be our ball."

"I know that," he said.

"I thought you didn't like football."

"I never said I didn't understand it. I just said I didn't watch it."

"That's okay, Nick," Betty said, sitting on the floor near the television with her ten-year old son beside her.

"If my home team was the New England Patriots, I wouldn't watch football either."

Everyone laughed, but Ray protested. "They'll do better next season. They've just had a run of bad luck."

Sarah grinned. "You sound like a die-hard fan, Ray. Do you go to any of the games?"

Nick answered for his friend. "He gave up his season tickets years ago when they got rid of the cheerleaders."

Janet looked at him. "You did what?"

Ray shrugged. "It was my way of protesting. I liked the cheerleaders."

Fin agreed. "Yeah, Ray. I know what you mean."

"Halftime!" Sarah saw the Cornhuskers jog off the football field and stood up. "I hope you're all hungry because Nick's meatballs are ready."

"I'll help you set it up," Janet said.

Betty got up off the floor. "Me, too."

"Okay." There wasn't much left to do except put the food on the table. Sarah had decorated the dining room table as she always did: a red tablecloth and a football, mounted on a pedestal, in the middle of the table. Red paper plates, Cornhusker napkins and silverware were off to one side, leaving plenty of room for the food. Sarah turned back to the men, who hadn't moved from their positions in front of the television. "You men can do the traditional routine and talk about cheerleaders while we put the food out. Who wants another beer?" Four hands went up. "I'll bring some out."

"You're a good woman, Sarah," Fin said.

"Remember that on Monday and take my class an extra ten minutes, will you?"

After she'd set four beers on the coffee table, Sarah returned to the kitchen and helped Janet and Betty remove dishes from the refrigerator. She found a large pottery bowl and started scooping meatballs into it.

"What else can I do?"

"You can take the rolls out of the bags and put them in the baskets."

"Okay." Betty unwrapped the bag. "Nick is gorgeous."

"Yes, I know."

Janet shook her head. "You two had better keep your voices down. They could hear you."

"With the TV blasting like that? I doubt it."

"He's gorgeous and he can cook and he's single. Do you think he's straight?"

Sarah remembered the way he'd flirted with her yesterday. "Yes."

"Do you know for sure?"

"Betty!"

"You're blushing."

"It's a family curse," Janet replied.

"Okay, Sarah, I won't tease you any more," Betty promised. "But he does seem like such a nice man."

"He is," Janet agreed. "We're all having such a good time this week."

Sarah grinned. "Especially you, Aunt Janet. Are you going to tell me what's going on?"

"Ray and I are just friends, dear. And that's all it could ever be."

"Is that what Ray thinks, too?"

"We haven't talked about it." Janet opened the refrigerator again and pulled out two bottles of root beer. "I bought extra for Billy," she said, "but I forgot to tell him to help himself."

Sarah realized the subject had been changed. She turned to Betty who shrugged.

"I'll tell the guys the food is ready," Betty offered. She picked up the baskets of rolls and headed out the door.

"You're not fooling anyone, Aunt Janet."

"I'm too old for romance," Janet replied. "I'm happy with the way my life has been."

"It's not over." Sarah lifted the bowl of meatballs. "There are worse things than falling in love."

"Speak for yourself, dear. You're the one who has her whole life ahead of her. One of these days you're going to have to put what happened behind you. There are a lot of good men out there, Sarah. You should start taking a chance on one."

"I think I'd rather watch football." She winked at her aunt. "It's a whole lot safer."

"Sometimes safety isn't all it's cracked up to be."

Sarah shook her head and turned toward the dining room. "I'm happy with the way things are, Aunt Janet."

WHEN THE LAST FOOTBALL FAN had left, Ray and Janet announced they were going to take a walk. "Don't do a thing around here," Janet ordered Sarah. "We'll all pitch in as soon as we get back."

Sarah didn't intend to pay a bit of attention to that particular order. "Sure," she told the departing couple. "Take your time."

As soon as they were out the door, Sarah picked up the peanut bowls from the coffee table and Nick grabbed the empty beer bottles. "You don't have to do this," she told him. "Why don't you go with Ray and Janet?"

He followed her out of the living room, through the dining room and into the kitchen. "I think they'd prefer to be alone again, don't you?"

Sarah put the bowls in the sink and eyed the mess on the island countertop. "They've been talking for four days. What else could they have to say?"

"I don't know," Nick said. "I've tried to find out how long Ray plans to stay, but he won't discuss it. He just smiles and tells me to relax."

"Janet won't even talk about it. What do you think is going on?"

"If they fell in love in 1942—"

"*If.*"

"It's beginning to look that way, Sarah. Whether you believe it or not." He folded his arms in front of him. "If they fell in love in 1942, then they could do it again. Fifty-one years later. Maybe that's what's happening now."

"I can't picture Janet with anyone but Uncle Jim."

"And I've never seen Ray this happy before." Sarah frowned, a worried expression clouding her hazel eyes. "Don't look like that," Nick said gently. "They'll work it out, sooner or later."

Sarah smiled. "Sooner would be nice."

"Tell me about it," he grinned. "I've called the office every day. For now they're managing just fine, but it can't go on forever."

"Next week is Thanksgiving."

Nick definitely did not want to talk about Thanksgiving. It was one of his least favorite holidays. "By the way, Sarah, that was quite a football party."

"Does that mean you're a Nebraska fan?"

Nick scraped the last bit of sauce from the pot and dumped it in the garbage. "I'm sure if I lived around here I would have to be, just as a matter of self-defense."

"You should see a game in person. It's *really* exciting."

"Today wasn't bad, although I was a little surprised when the basket of potato chips went up in the air."

"Betty got a little carried away. I don't think she knew she had the basket in her hand when she started to cheer."

"At least they beat Oklahoma, and we still have a shot at the Orange Bowl."

"See? You're starting to sound like a Nebraskan."

"Oh, I don't think so." He laughed.

"You looked like one." She took the dirty pot and plunged it into the sinkful of soapy water. "And everyone loved the food."

"Well, your red gelatin was a hit, too."

"That's another tradition."

"So I gathered."

"Seriously, Nick, thanks for helping out."

Nick stepped closer and leaned against the counter. His dark gaze held hers. "It's the least I can do. I never thought we'd still be here four days later, but it's been fun. Ray's never forced me to take a vacation before."

"Where do you usually go on your vacation?"

"I don't. Ray and I keep pretty busy. We'd wanted to try the Colorado slopes, but that didn't work out. Ray was pretty anxious to come to North Platte first."

"Why don't you go anyway?"

"He's still my boss. If he wants me to be here, then I'm here. Besides, after that scene with his chest pains, I'd feel strange leaving him alone."

Sarah thought of the scares she'd had with Janet. "I know what you mean. I know how I'd feel if anything happened to my aunt."

"What about the rest of your family?"

"My parents are both dead. There are two other aunts, my father's sisters, one west of town and another in Lincoln. And Aunt Mary Anne, in Omaha. Plus an assortment of cousins. Most of them will be here next week." She rinsed the pot and set it in the second sink to drain while Nick slid a platter into the soapy water. Sarah turned back, bumping into his hard chest as she automatically reached into the sink.

"Excuse—" she began, but Nick touched her chin and lifted it slightly so she had to look up at him. Had to look up into those gorgeous dark eyes of his as he bent down to touch his lips to hers.

A small kiss, it still was like an electric shock. Sarah couldn't move, her hands helpless in the water, as his lips touched hers again in a silent question. She closed her eyes against the sensual onslaught and kissed him back, despite all the warning bells going off in her head. His fingers slid from her chin and into her hair, holding her still for his kiss. She couldn't have moved if she wanted to. And she didn't want to. When Nick finally lifted his lips, Sarah didn't know whether to be relieved or disappointed.

Surprised, definitely. Certain she looked like an amazed adolescent, Sarah recovered quickly. "I think everything but the clay platters will fit in the dishwasher," she said, hoping she didn't sound too shaken up.

"Sarah," he began, his voice low. "Should I apologize?"

She looked back at him and smiled. "Of course not."

"Good." His brown eyes twinkled at her. "Because I intend to kiss you again." He looked down at the sink. "Why don't you take your hands out of the water and put them around my neck?"

"No way."

"Afraid?" he challenged, a thread of laughter in his voice.

"You're a born flirt," Sarah replied, turning to give her attention to washing the bowls. "And I'm not going to encourage you."

"Oh, sweetheart, you already have."

She shot him a look designed to put a stop to his teasing, but he didn't seem at all bothered. In fact, the grin he gave her was anything but contrite. Sarah looked away, determined to resist his easy charm from now on. She wasn't going to let him see how that kiss had affected her. Underneath the water she gripped the sponge and started scrubbing.

"It's still early," Nick said, picking up a dish towel and reaching for the pot. "We could go out. There has to be a movie theater in town, isn't there?"

Sarah turned on the faucet and rinsed the bowls. "You think Ray and Janet are up to that?"

"I'm not asking Ray and Janet. I'm asking you."

"Thanks, but—"

The back door opened and the older couple stepped in and shut the door with a solid bang. Janet hurried up the steps and rounded the corner. "I told you they wouldn't wait for us to help, Ray. We should have come back sooner."

"No," Sarah assured her, thinking of Nick's kiss. "You came back at just the right time."

Nick tossed the dish towel onto the counter. "I'm trying to talk Sarah into seeing a movie tonight."

Janet smiled. "What a good idea!"

"Would you like to come, too?" Sarah squeezed the excess water from the sponge and started scrubbing drops of tomato sauce from the stove.

Ray spoke for them. "Not tonight, but thanks for asking. It's been a long day."

Janet turned to him with a worried expression. "Are you feeling all right?"

"I'm fine. But I don't intend to go out in that cold again."

"We could rent a movie," Sarah offered. "That way we could all see it."

"That's not—" Nick began.

"Didn't you want to see *Enchanted April*, Aunt Janet?"

"Well, yes, but—"

"Great." Sarah turned back to Nick and plastered a smile on her face. "Do you mind going to the video store?"

"You come and show me the way."

"It's right down the street. You can't miss—"

"Come on," he ordered, taking her elbow. "We'll let the old folks finish up in here."

Ray grinned. "You did most of it. I think we got off easy."

Sarah figured she'd gotten off pretty easy herself. She'd successfully avoided a date with the Italian lady-killer.

So why was she disappointed?

Once they were in the car and heading out of the driveway, Nick said, "Nice move."

"What?"

"The movie-rental maneuver. Why didn't you want to go out with me?"

She wasn't about to tell him he scared her to death. It wasn't him exactly though, she realized, but her reaction to him. "What's the point?"

"I thought we could at least enjoy ourselves since we're here together. It just seemed natural."

"Natural?"

"To be friends," he explained patiently, glancing over at her before he turned back to watch the road in front of him. He turned right and headed toward the interstate before he added, "Or more."

Sarah decided to ignore that. "Is this another one of your plans to leave Janet and Ray alone?"

"He does enjoy that."

"And is this part of your job description?"

"Maybe." He smiled at her in the darkness as they waited for the red light to turn to green. "Or maybe it's just part of being a friend."

"What does Ray want, anyway?"

The light changed and Nick stepped on the gas. "I'm beginning to be afraid I know the answer," he muttered.

SARAH HURRIED UPSTAIRS to the two rooms on the south side of the second-floor hallway that belonged to her in the winter. A bathroom connected them, so Janet moved out of the master bedroom in the summer and she and Sarah enjoyed their privacy while the guests used the bathroom at the end of the hall. During the off-season, Sarah used the extra room as an office. Tonight she should have been correcting English compositions instead of watching *Under Siege*. She'd enjoyed the look of surprise on Nick's face when she'd selected the action-packed thriller plus the movie she'd known Janet had wanted to see.

"The kids turned me on to these movies," she'd admitted. "And I like them. Or most of them. I'll watch anything but horror movies."

"We finally have something in common," he'd said, his dark eyes flashing.

Oh, they had a lot in common. That's what bothered her. Sarah pulled out her desk chair and eyed the stack of papers waiting for her. Instead she thought of Nick's kiss, of the tempting pressure of his lips on hers. Definitely exciting. Definitely enjoyable.

Definitely dangerous.

She opened the top drawer of the desk and pulled out a tiny silver frame. A baby's face, her eyes closed and the tiny tufts of hair she was born with sticking up, peered back at her. A beautiful child, and a reminder that love didn't always last. That promises weren't forever, no matter how much one prayed for a Christmas miracle.

Christmas was coming, and Sarah knew better than to dwell on the past. She put the picture back in the drawer and shut it with a firm push. She had plenty to keep her busy, including the Christmas program, the usual holiday shopping and the Thanksgiving dinner to plan. Nick Ciminero was the least of her worries. So she'd kissed him. Big deal. She was lonely, she admitted it. Maybe she should say yes the next time Fin asked her out.

As for Nick, she'd treat him as a friend, just as she did with the other men in her life. She could ignore the tremendous physical attraction if she simply tried harder. And that's what she would do from now on. No matter how much his dark eyes tempted her otherwise.

"YOU'RE UP EARLY," Ray said, sipping his coffee at the kitchen table. "You even beat the women. Why are you all dressed up?"

"We need to talk," Nick said, pouring himself a cup of coffee, careful not to splatter any on his white shirt and paisley silk tie. "I need to get out of here."

"You're going back to Providence?"

Nick shook his head, surprised by the shock in Ray's voice. "No. I want to head to Denver for a few days. There aren't any snowstorms heading this way, so I shouldn't have any trouble. We barely scratched the surface there, you know. And I'm getting edgy."

Ray frowned. "I wanted you to have a vacation. You can't make work your whole life, son."

Nick shrugged. "I've never had anything else, Ray, and you know it. It's all I know."

"Well," the old man grumped. "Know something else."

Nick laughed. "Just because you're happy to sit around here doesn't mean I am. And I refuse to go to Rhode Island without you. You may never return and I'll be left trying to explain to everyone that the boss is in Nebraska and isn't coming home. What would happen then?"

"That's not far from the truth—"

Nick raised his hand. "No. I don't want to hear it. Just tell me when we're leaving. It'll have to be soon. After all, Thanksgiving is this week."

"I've been giving that some thought. Neither one of us has any family left."

"Last year we went out for dinner and then came back to your place and watched the football games. It wasn't bad."

"You worked at the computer all afternoon. I watched the games. I don't call that much of a holiday."

"It was enough for me."

Ray made a face. "It's not enough for me anymore. If Janet invites me to stay, I'm going to say yes. I'll let you decide what you want to do."

EASY FOR THE OLD MAN to say, Nick thought, heading west on Interstate 80. He had three or four hours to think about Thanksgiving and his own unrealistic attraction to Sarah McGrath. She wasn't anything like the women he usually dated—not sleek or sophisticated. She was more honest, outspoken . . . and interesting.

And she didn't seem at all interested in him. Except for the kiss, which she'd responded to. Then she'd backed off again, as if she'd regained her senses. She'd treated him like a friend, which, come to think of it, was the way she treated that giant Fin and the shy music teacher.

It was good to get away, Nick decided, watching the wide open spaces pass by at sixty-five miles an hour. He needed to get back to work, to do what he knew best, which was figure out how to make money.

He switched on the radio and turned it to an all-news station. He needed more reality in his life right now. He needed something to think about other than the sweet taste of Sarah's lips against his.

6

JANET LOOKED FORWARD to breakfast with him. After Jim's death, evenings weren't as lonely as they could have been—not with Sarah around to keep her company while she watched television. She'd knit and Sarah would spread her schoolwork around the couch. But mornings were a different story since Sarah left early, and the only thing to greet an old woman was a half-filled coffeepot.

Now there was Ray. Handsome, strong and stubborn Ray. So different from her husband and yet, as she watched him read the paper with the concentration of a lawyer, maybe not so different.

It was good to have a man around in the mornings. He didn't expect her to wait on him, and even grumbled when she did, but she enjoyed it. And he enjoyed it, too, she was sure of that. Even after all these years, she knew him well enough to know he'd have been on the next plane out of North Platte if he didn't want to be here any longer.

It was good to have a man behind the wheel of her car. He liked to drive her around on her errands. His interest in old cooking gadgets led her to more antique shops than she'd ever visited before. He seemed to enjoy exploring the countryside, and so far there hadn't been any snow to stop them.

They'd been lucky. For once.

Janet poured herself another cup of coffee and took it over to the table. Ray dropped his newspaper and smiled at her as she sat down across from him.

"What do you want to do today?" he asked.

"It's Sunday. I have church at ten-thirty."

"I'll take you, if you wouldn't mind."

"A group of us go out to dinner after church. Would you like to join us?"

He hesitated, then nodded. "Sure, Janet. Unless you think it would be awkward."

"Why would it be awkward? You're an old friend. They'd love to meet you."

Ray looked at her, but Janet couldn't read the expression in his dark eyes. She couldn't tell what he was thinking, which, come to think of it, had been part of the problem so many years ago. But she wasn't going to think about that, she reminded herself. The past couldn't be fixed now.

"I want to be more than an old friend," he said, slapping the paper down on the table.

Janet thought of the box of letters stored in her closet. "We're too old for that."

"No, we're not," he argued, taking her hand in his. "Shall I prove it to you?"

Janet almost blushed, but the touch of his hand on hers warmed her more than she thought possible. "Ray," she stammered. "Don't embarrass me."

"I'm not trying to. I'm just stating the truth." His eyes darkened as he looked at her and rubbed his thumb along the palm of her hand. "I've wanted you since that Christmas Eve fifty years ago, and I still want you."

"Fifty years is a long time."

"An eternity, a blink of an eye, I don't know." He looked at her with eyes filled with love. "I only know that you and I are together now, and I'm grateful."

Janet shook her head, as if to deny such feelings still existed. "So much has happened. We're two different people."

"No, not really. You're the same sweet, gentle girl I remember. The same girl I fell in love with then, and I'm falling in love with now."

"Ray," she began, searching for the words to tell him how she felt. "It's too late for us."

"If I believed that I would never have come back."

"Why did you, Ray? Why now, after all this time?"

"A heart attack makes a man think about his life, Janet. Even a mild attack like the one I had was a warning. Nick never knew—he was off on a business trip at the time—and I managed to keep it quiet with the rest of the people who work for me. But it's not something I can forget. Like I've never forgotten you. *Peaches and cream*, that's what I thought when I first saw you. I always called you Peaches in my letters, remember?"

"Memories are fine, Raymond. But at our age—"

"We're not dead, Janet, just in our sixties."

"Almost seventies."

"So? I can still make love to you."

Janet tried to pull her hand away. "You said you wouldn't embarrass me."

He sighed. "All right." He released her hand. "Are you going to make me leave?"

"Of course not." Janet knew the goodbyes would come soon enough. She didn't have to force it.

"Thanksgiving is this Thursday."

"I know. I have a million things to do to get ready."

"We'll leave when Nick returns from Denver."

The disappointment was sharp, a pain right through her chest. "Why would you leave? And why did Nick go to Denver?"

"It's just for a couple of days. The boy got restless and had to go think up some work." He reached over and folded the newspaper into a neat rectangle before he stood up. "I'd better get ready or we'll be late for church."

He picked up his empty coffee cup and took it over to the sink, and Janet followed him. "Ray," she said, making him turn around. "Stay for Thanksgiving. Unless your family would be disappointed if you weren't there."

His smile took her breath away. "I'd love to stay," he said, reaching out to cup her chin with his large hand. "There is no one who matters in my life more than you."

"You shouldn't say that."

Ray slid his fingers along her cheek and bent over to touch his lips to hers for one brief moment. "I can say anything I want," he said, his lips curving into a smile. He kissed her again, this time with a more insistent pressure, and Janet reached for his shoulders as if she'd been kissing him all of her life. When he released her, his dark eyes twinkled. "See?" he said, "We're not too old after all."

Janet watched him leave the kitchen before she turned back to the counter and stared at the loaf of bread in front of her. What had she done—kissing Ray and inviting him to stay for Thanksgiving? Sarah was never going to understand.

"MISS MCGRATH! Miss McGrath!"

Sarah looked up from the sheaf of papers and saw Mary Sawyer waving her arm. "Yes, Mary?"

"There's someone knocking on the door."

"Turn the music down," Sarah ordered, and a heavyset boy with a tape player complied as Sarah went to the door of her room. Anyone who wanted to rehearse more had volunteered to stay after school and work on their lines, but the noise level had necessitated the door being kept shut at all times.

"We need a song after the Ghost of Christmas Past does his thing," one child said, following Sarah to the door. "Us boys want to use a Vanilla Ice tape and the girls want some guy with long hair to sing some totally dumb song."

"Give me a minute, then we'll play the songs and decide which one is most fitting." Sarah wondered why she had ever thought that *A Christmas Carol* should be rewritten as a play by fifth-graders. And why she'd agreed to a musical version, too.

"Great!" Tony grinned at her. "This is gonna be *so cool*, Miss McGrath, you're not gonna believe it!"

Sarah couldn't help but grin back. Each year she thought she had the best group of children, and then the next year gave her another wonderful class. Tony, who had started off the year as a shy little boy, had taken over the musical direction of the show with the aplomb of Tommy Tune.

She'd almost reached the door when it opened. Sarah expected the masculine hand that held the doorknob to belong to the principal, but instead Nick's face greeted her as she looked up, ready to apologize for the noise. 'Nick?"

"Hi." He stepped inside the room and Sarah hurried to shut the door behind him. "I hope you don't mind, but Janet said you were staying after school today to rehearse."

"Well, no, but I—"

"Didn't expect me back so soon?" He shrugged off his coat. "The forecast was for snow this evening, so I decided I'd better head back here before I got stuck in Denver."

"But why are you here?"

"I thought I'd drive you home." Which was only a small part of the truth. He'd missed her, and when Janet suggested he pick Sarah up at school he'd jumped at the chance. Nick looked around the classroom and twenty-one pairs of eyes looked back. "Is there anything I can do to help?"

Sarah told herself it was ridiculous to feel so pleased. She took a deep breath. "I'll introduce you." She clapped her hands together and announced, "I'd like you to meet a friend of mine, Mr. Ciminero. He's going to watch some of the rehearsal, so why don't you take advantage of having an audience and we'll run through the first act again?"

Tony sidled up to her. "What about the music?"

"Let's discuss that later on, after we do the first act."

Tony glared at Nick and moved away. The girls giggled as they pushed the front row of desks back a few feet and took their places at the front of the room. "Now, Miss McGrath?"

"Now." Sarah motioned for Nick to sit down in one of the vacant seats, so he sat on top of the desk next to her. She hid her smile as she watched the girls preen for Nick's benefit. "Okay, start!" The nine girls stared back at her. "Start with, 'It will soon be Christmas,' all right? Annabelle?"

Annabelle shook her fluffy yellow hair and nodded. Striking a pose, she trilled, "It will soon be Christmas, and time for all of us to finish our shopping." She looked first at Nick, then at her teacher. "How was that?"

"Just fine. Keep going." The rest of the girls giggled. "Quiet, everyone. You have to get used to doing this in front of people, so get a grip."

Annabelle sighed dramatically. "I'll start over. 'It will soon be Christmas, and time for all of us to finish our shopping.'" The rest of the girls chimed in, and after a few minutes Jimmy Dorset swaggered past them as Scrooge, mumbling his lines and making the girls giggle again.

"Jimmy, start over again," Sarah directed. "And speak just a little slower, please. After all, you're the star of the show."

That pleased him. He gave Nick a suspicious look, then grinned at his beloved Miss McGrath. "Yeah. Okay. *Bah, humbug!*"

It didn't get any better, but at least it didn't get any worse, Sarah decided as she watched the children say their lines. A couple of times they stopped and conferred, then hurried to make changes in the dialogue. After twenty minutes, Sarah could tell they'd had enough.

"We'd better stop now. Besides, your parents will be waiting for you." Sarah looked out the window and noticed the snowflakes falling. "It looks like we might have a storm coming."

The children started grabbing their coats. Tony hurried over with his tape recorder. He popped the tape out and handed it to her. "Here, Miss McGrath, you can take it home and see what you think."

"Wonderful, Tony. Thanks."

"You're welcome."

He looked over at Nick. "Do you live around here?"

"No. I'm from Rhode Island."

Jimmy Dorset snorted. "Rhode Island? What kinda place is that?"

"A small one." Nick stood up and picked up his coat.

"Yeah," Jimmy agreed. "I knew that."

"You a teacher or somethin'?" Tommy asked.

"No."

"Then why are you here?"

"I heard about your play and I wanted to see for myself."

That stunned the two boys. Even the girls, who had come closer to listen to what the stranger was talking to the boys about, looked astonished.

"Well," one of the boys finally ventured. "What do ya think?"

Nick looked thoughtful, as if giving the question great consideration. "It has a lot of possibilities. You wrote it yourself?" They nodded. "I'm impressed. I hope I can see the rest of it."

"You can come back tomorrow," Annabelle offered, slinging her purple backpack over her shoulder. "When are we practicing, Miss McGrath?"

"Not until Monday. Tomorrow we're baking pumpkin pies, remember?" Sarah put her coat on, wound her bright scarf around her neck and picked up her tote bag.

"I'll carry that," Nick offered, taking the heavy canvas bag out of her hand.

"Thanks." He looked very sophisticated in his unbuttoned wool coat, ivory pullover and charcoal corduroy slacks. He was the picture of country elegance, but he was going to freeze to death before he crossed the parking lot.

"You're baking pies?" he echoed. "The woman who doesn't cook?"

"I organize. The mothers bake," she explained, following the last child out the door and waiting for Nick to walk out so she could lock the door behind her. She hurried down the hall toward the main doors so she could make sure the children found their rides. "I suppose you're going to tell me you make Italian pumpkin pies."

"Not pumpkin. Spinach."

"You're teasing me, right?" Sarah pulled on her gloves and watched the children laughing outside on the snow-covered grass in front of the parking lot where parents waited to take them home.

"I'm very serious," he argued, but the laughter in his voice couldn't be disguised. "They're folded crescents or triangles of dough with spinach and pepperoni inside, then baked. You can eat them hot or cold."

"Like runzas."

"Runzas?"

"A Nebraska specialty," she explained. "Hamburger and cabbage baked in dough."

"I'd like to try one."

"Janet makes them every once in a while. You should ask her."

"I'll get the recipe."

She noticed he didn't commit himself to staying long enough for Janet to make them. Maybe he was leaving tomorrow, although this storm might make that impossible. "You might need a little Polish in you in order to make them," she teased.

"I can pretend. After all, who knows?"

She looked at his thick dark hair and gorgeous olive skin. "No, I think you're very much Italian. You and Ray are very much alike."

"How is he doing? No more attacks while I was away?"

"No. He's been fine, as far as I know. He and Janet are practically inseparable. They act like an old married couple half the time."

"Yeah. I noticed that, too. They suggested I give you a ride home."

"I'm glad."

"Glad because you don't have to walk in the snow or glad to see me?"

She tipped her head so she could look in his eyes. Tempted to tease him, she hesitated. "Maybe a little of both. How was Denver? I envy you."

He held the door open for her and they both gasped as the frigid air hit their faces. "Why?"

She bent her head down and they hurried across the lawn to the parking area. She didn't answer until they were both tucked inside the car. It still held a little warmth. "Because," she said, "it's one of my favorite places."

"You ski?"

"I used to. Whenever I got the chance."

"See?" He started the ignition. "We have something else in common."

"What else?"

"Ray. Janet. Food."

"Nebraska football?"

"It could grow on me."

She laughed, and it felt good. She didn't stop to think why she was in such a good mood. Of course, rehearsals had gone well, math had proceeded without any trouble and her book order had arrived this morning. Surely this surprising happiness couldn't have anything to do with Nicholas Ciminero returning from Denver.

"So," he said, turning the car onto Fourth Street. "What's new in North Platte?"

"Uh-oh. You haven't heard?"

"Heard what?"

"Ray is staying for Thanksgiving." She watched his handsome, etched profile as he slowly drove along the street, peering between the windshield wipers as the snow came down faster and faster. He didn't say anything. "You're not surprised?"

"Not really."

"But what about you? What do you want to do?"

"You mean about Thanksgiving?"

"Yes. You're included in the invitation, of course."

Nick didn't say anything. The only sound in the car was the hot air blasting from the vents. "I'll give it some thought," he said, keeping his eyes on the road. He didn't sound happy about the invitation.

Sarah decided to change the subject. What did it matter to her whether or not Nick stayed for the holiday? "Did you finish your business in Denver?"

"No, but I know what I need to learn." He turned right, pulled the car into the driveway and parked in front of the door. The snow, heavier now, surrounded them. Nick turned the ignition off and it was suddenly very quiet. Sarah put her hand on the door and started to open it, anxious to escape the hushed intimacy of the car. He was too close, too appealing and altogether too dangerous to be around. She could handle it when they were together in the large brick house or surrounded by schoolchildren, but the inside of the gray sedan was almost suffocating.

Nick seemed as anxious to get out of the car as she did, grabbing the heavy tote bag as he opened his door and stepped out into the cold afternoon air. They stopped at the front steps, but as Sarah put her hand on the brass door handle, Nick touched her hand to stop her.

"Sarah," he began, then stopped and looked down at her. A tiny crystal snowflake caught her eyelash as she looked up at him, a question in her eyes. A little apprehension, too.

"What?"

"Thanksgiving," he said, watching as she blinked the tiny crystal drop, but three more took its place. "I hate it."

"Oh. I've never met anyone who hated Thanksgiving before."

"I'm not crazy about Christmas, either."

"Neither am I," she admitted, and he didn't miss the flash of pain in her eyes or the tightening of her mouth. He couldn't take his gaze away from her mouth, all soft and pink. He could see her breath, little puffs of air, in the dim light.

"Guess we're two Scrooges," he murmured, bending closer to her and dropping the bag onto the brick step. "Will you tell me why?"

She stepped toward him as he put his hands on her shoulders and held her. He began to lower his head to hers.

"No," she said. He stopped himself short and instead of tasting her lips, he felt the warmth of her breath, smelled the faint floral perfume.

"No?" She was warm and willing in his arms.

"No to the question." She put her arms around his neck and touched her lips to his. "Yes to—"

He cut off her words with his lips. *Yes* was what he wanted, needed to hear. Her lips were warm, her skin cool as his fingers found her face and held her still. He didn't know how much he'd missed her until he tasted her, felt the tiny tremble of her lower lip against his tongue as he parted her mouth. She was soft and sweet and everything he thought she would be, everything he'd fantasized about for three days, since the first time he'd kissed her. He pulled her closer, slanting his mouth against her to plunge deeper, to taste and touch and take the inside of her mouth as if he was taking all of her with his body.

She didn't pull away, but seemed to hesitate, almost as if she was waiting to see what he would do next. She held back, and he slowed down to give her time to respond. She met him with answering passion and heat. He tasted icy bits of snow as he lifted his mouth a fraction of an inch from hers, could feel the moisture on his eyelashes. Sarah's mittened hands were still on his shoulders, and she touched the tip of her tongue to a snowflake that had paused on the corner of Nick's mouth.

His body quivered in response to the gentle exploration, and he held himself still as she kissed snowflakes from his jaw, moving up to his earlobe and back down again to find new drops on his lips.

"I like snow," she murmured.

"My turn," he said. He'd become unaware of the cold. His body was on fire, and he knew hers was, too. He touched a snowflake on her upper lip, the tip of his tongue immediately melting it into a tiny drop he tasted and forgot. He couldn't wait for snowflakes, but took her mouth in an embrace that should have melted the snow from both their bodies and steamed the ancient bricks beneath their feet.

Nick didn't know how long they stood there, but it wasn't long enough. He could have kissed her for hours, for days, if he'd had the freedom. He wanted to memorize each silky inch of her mouth, wanted to feel her body pressed against his and unbutton her clothing layer by layer, fold by fold until he found the waiting skin to tease and touch with his fingers and taste with his mouth. He moved his hands to her neck, wanting to strip the woolly scarf from her neck and move his lips to the skin beneath her earlobe, wanting to begin unwrapping the package that was Sarah McGrath. She shivered, whether in reaction to his lips or the snowstorm, Nick didn't know.

He lifted his head and looked down into her hazel eyes. "You're cold."

She shook her head, causing snowflakes to cascade onto her shoulders. "No. I'm scared."

Nick tugged her against him, wrapping his arms around her and hugging her against his wide chest. "Who was he?"

She knew what he meant. "It was a long time ago."

"Tell me."

"No. It doesn't have anything to do with you."

He looked down at her, needing to see her face. "It does if it makes you afraid, Sarah."

"It's not you," she said once again, and Nick couldn't resist touching her lips with his and taking her mouth one more time. *Only a moment more*, he promised himself. *Then we'll go inside and pretend nothing happened.*

"Sarah? I—" Janet's voice trailed off as Nick broke away from the kiss and turned to look at the woman standing in the open door. Janet blushed. "I'm sorry, I heard the car drive up but when you didn't come in I wondered if something was wrong."

Sarah picked up her tote bag and brushed past Nick toward the open door. "Nothing's wrong, Aunt Janet," she managed to say as she entered the warm foyer and stood on the thick yellow rug. "We should have come in the back so we wouldn't track snow."

"Nonsense," the older woman replied, watching Sarah carefully. "You always used the front door when you were a little girl. You said it made you feel important. It doesn't make any difference at all, and you know it. How was the rehearsal?"

"Just fine. I was glad to have the ride home, though."

Ray looked up from his seat on the couch. "Hello, you two. Are we in for a storm?"

Nick shut the door behind him and helped Sarah remove her coat before taking off his own coat and gloves. Any excuse to touch her, he realized. "It's just beginning, I think. Have you heard the weather report?" Nick didn't listen to Ray's reply. He didn't care about the weather. He wished he could take Sarah upstairs and forget about the storm, just tuck her into his bed on the third floor and not reappear for days until they'd made love so many times that they'd memorized the feel of each other's skin.

Instead he hung the coats in the nearby closet and accepted Janet's offer of hot chocolate and freshly baked pound cake. He wasn't going to leave Sarah, not just yet. Even if that meant he was stuck here for Thanksgiving.

"YOU'RE AWFULLY QUIET, dear."

Sarah put the dirty cups in the sink. "It was a long day."

"Is he staying for the weekend?"

She knew that "he" didn't refer to Ray. "I don't know. He's not crazy about Thanksgiving."

Janet nodded. "I can understand that."

"Why?"

"Well, it has to do with his family, I suppose. Forget I said anything." Janet smiled. "Don't look so surprised. He's a nice young man and we've had some time to talk."

"About what?"

Janet shrugged and grabbed her apron. "A lot of things. He's an ambitious young man with quite a future ahead of him, but he doesn't strike me as the kind of man who would deliberately hurt another person."

"Meaning me."

"Yes. He looks at you as if he can't figure you out."

He kisses that way, too, Sarah wanted to say. "Okay, Aunt Janet, I confess that I like him. Very much. But that's all there is to it. We have two different lives in two different parts of the country. It's not like he lives next door. There's nothing but a little mutual attraction, nothing else."

"It looked like there was more to it than that on the steps a little while ago."

"I knew you would bring that up."

"Well, of course. It was so romantic with the snow falling all around and you wrapped in Nick's arms and—"

"Aunt Janet!"

"All right, I'll mind my own business from now on." She smiled one of her all-knowing smiles and left the kitchen, leaving Sarah to ponder a sink full of sticky cups.

It had been wonderful kissing Nick. She'd wanted to, would have been disappointed if he hadn't kissed her when he'd taken her in his strong arms and touched her face. He'd acted as if she was fragile, then kissed her with a demanding passionate force that should have sent them both tumbling into the shrubbery. She'd been too surprised then to wonder at her reaction, but in the quiet room she wondered suddenly if there was more to this than just the simple physical attraction between a man and a woman.

She liked the way he looked at her. Liked the simple strength in him, and the enthusiasm he put into cooking. There was a protectiveness, too, which surprised her. Sarah McGrath didn't think she needed protecting, but she wasn't complaining when he tucked her into the car and saved her a wet walk home. Or when he touched her as if he thought she would break.

But she didn't have anything to give a man like that.

"I HEAR you're staying for Thanksgiving." Nick leaned against the doorframe and waited for Ray to finish buttoning his new black-and-white plaid shirt. "When did you start wearing flannel shirts?"

"Since Janet picked it out," he replied. "And I like the look."

Nick shook his head. "Don't go getting weird on me, Ray. We have a seven-million-dollar business to run, remember?"

"I remember. I call the office at least once, sometimes twice a day. Everything is going fine."

"That's because *I'm* calling five times a day and answering questions and returning the important calls." Nick ran his hand through his hair, leaving the dark waves tousled. "I don't know how much longer we can continue to stay here. We've been gone two weeks already."

"You've never liked Thanksgiving. Why do you care where we spend it?"

"I—"

"And besides, you'd have Thursday through Sunday off anyway. Pretend you're in Rhode Island." He turned to Nick and chuckled. "Although you couldn't stand around kissing Sarah in Rhode Island, could you?"

"I really don't want to talk—"

"Janet told me." Ray's brown eye's twinkled. "It's hard to resist these Nebraska women, isn't it, son?"

"Yes," Nick answered. "It is."

"I don't think you're as upset about staying here as you pretend to be. If you're so fired up to get back to work, go right ahead." Ray waved toward the hallway. "Pack your bags and fly home. You don't have to worry about me, Niccolo."

Nick stared at Ray as he picked up a brush and fixed his hair in the gilded mirror above the dresser, but he wasn't paying attention. He was thinking of Sarah and remembering how she felt in his arms. He'd done a lot of thinking while he drove to Denver and back. It might be time to settle down, have children. It might be time to buy that five-bedroom oceanfront home he'd driven past countless times.

He sure as hell hadn't intended to fall in love, but now that he thought about it, it might not be that terrible a thing if he did. He could do a lot worse than fall in love with Sarah McGrath, an outspoken woman with a tender heart and a unique way of removing snowflakes.

7

THERE WAS NO PEACE to be found in the brick house on Fourth Street the day before Thanksgiving. Ray walked into the kitchen early that morning, expecting his usual quiet breakfast-for-two with the love of his life and instead discovered Janet studying a twenty-three-pound turkey. It grew obvious that she was more enthusiastic about the Thanksgiving dinner menu than sitting with Ray at the table and discussing the weather, politics, or their plans for the day.

"Good morning." He hoped she'd move away from the counter and into his arms, but she didn't. "What are you staring at?"

"My list for Thanksgiving dinner."

He peered over her shoulder. He recognized the handwriting, and the sight of her neatly formed letters took his breath and threw it back down to his lungs. Suddenly he was nineteen, with strong hands and young fingers that carefully opened the envelopes addressed to him. The envelopes with the return address of North Platte, Nebraska, and addressed to a homesick medic. He'd fallen in love with Janet and her beautiful capital S. Those days seemed so long ago now, and yet the sight of her handwriting could still make his heart beat faster with joy. He tried to say something normal. "What are you having for dinner?"

"Traditional turkey, oyster dressing, potatoes, gravy, squash, cranberry sauce, and pies," she answered. "And an assortment of other things, too."

"Are you doing all of the cooking?"

"Oh, no, of course not." She consulted a list on the counter. "Everyone brings something. My cousin Laura is doing a couple of pies, Mary Anne the salads, and my Aunt Esther—bless her heart—always brings a turnip casserole."

"Which leaves you with the turkey, dressing, potatoes, gravy, squash, and cranberry sauce. How many people are you having?"

Janet frowned. "That's what I've been trying to figure out." She looked back at her paper. "Sarah invited some people from school, but I can't remember who she said was coming and who isn't. If everyone comes, counting us, there'll be twenty-four. Twenty-three if Nick leaves, but I have a feeling he's going to stay, don't you?"

Ray moved to the refrigerator and took out the milk. It was going to be a cold-cereal morning, but if he could get around the turkey he could make some toast. Janet had a seemingly unending supply of homemade jams and jellies that begged for toast.

"Don't you, Ray?" she repeated.

"Don't I what?"

"Think Nick is going to stay? I hate to think of him leaving now, when we're all going to have such a wonderful time."

"He's not going anywhere," Ray assured her, taking her shoulders and turning her toward him. He kissed her briefly, then smiled. "I'm the only family that boy has, and we're not even related."

Janet smiled back. "What about your family, Ray? Won't they miss you tomorrow?"

"There aren't that many Sandettis left," Ray said.

"Here, let me move the turkey. I'll keep you company while you have your breakfast. I'll work on the squash while you eat. You can tell me about your family's Thanksgivings."

"Thirty or forty people was a typical gathering for years in my mother's house. She was the oldest girl in the family and she always had the rest of the family for holidays. When she died, so many years ago, the rest of her sisters took turns having the family, but it was never the same. Now, with so many of the family dead or retired to California or Florida, there aren't many people left to celebrate a holiday with."

His father's people had clung to old traditions for years, until there were no more Sandettis—only himself, a bachelor—to make the pasta and the sauces and the antipasto and the canelloni and all the other delicacies that made a family gathering complete. "I would miss the food," Ray added. "But I sell it every day, it's my life."

It *was* his life, he realized. And yet, he hadn't missed it, not once, in the days he'd been with Janet.

"It's good to have work you love," Janet agreed. "But I look at Sarah and worry that it's all she has. Teaching is her life, but I wish she had a husband and children, too."

"She's a beautiful and talented girl," Ray said, waiting for his toast to pop up. "You shouldn't worry so much."

"What about Nick? He isn't married?"

"No."

"Divorced?"

"No. He never married." Ray put the toast on his plate and watched Janet open cans of yams. "Too wrapped up in the business, just like I was. Before you know it, time has gone by and you're alone at night with the television set."

She shot him a wry look. "Don't try to convince me that you didn't break a few hearts in the past fifty years, Raymond Sandetti. I don't believe you were a monk."

He grinned. "No. But I only gave my heart to one girl, and she broke it."

Janet's smile faded. "Don't talk about the past, Ray. And don't tease."

He stood closer and put his arms around her, cradling her head against his shoulder. "Why not, Jan? It's true."

"No. I never meant to hurt you. The past should stay just where it is, in the past."

Ray shook his head, knowing Janet couldn't see him disagree. "No, Peaches," he said. "Not when you get a second chance, it shouldn't."

"WOMEN ONLY," Sarah announced, barring the door to the kitchen. "We're busy in here."

Nick and Ray looked at her as if they couldn't believe they wouldn't be welcomed into the kitchen the afternoon before Thanksgiving. "We could help," Ray tried.

Sarah shook her head. "Thanks, but we don't need you in here getting underfoot."

"The woman underestimates us," Nick said. "I'm a chef, for heaven's sake."

Sarah tried not to laugh. "If you want to help, go get a couple of pizzas."

Ray took his arm and tugged him toward the foyer. "Son, you have a lot to learn about women. When they're busy planning a party, you'd better leave them alone. The best thing to do, the only way to survive, is to stay out of their way and don't make any mess anywhere else in the house. Oh," he said, remembering something else. "And don't use the good hand towels in the bathroom and don't eat anything off the trays until the company arrives."

Nick jammed his hands in his pockets. "I should have gone back to Providence. They're in the middle of the busiest time of the year."

"What do you think I pay everyone for? You've trained 'em well, and I've paid 'em well, too. I think they're glad we're both gone."

"Yes, well, you could be right. Mike didn't sound too upset. Just busy. I think he wants to prove he can handle it."

"And he will." Ray pulled the drapes back from the window and looked outside to the snow-covered lawn. "I had the boys pack up some of our best products and fly them out here. I keep thinking it'll show up soon." He turned to Nick and winked. "Our contribution to the feast tomorrow, you know. Now, who's going to get the pizza?"

"I will," Nick said, sighing.

"Cheer up, son."

"You know I've never liked this holiday." In this place he felt like an outsider, with that uncomfortable I'm-grateful-to-be-here-because-I-have-nowhere-else-to-go feeling. He hadn't felt this way in years, because he and Ray were two of a kind. Family, practically.

"You might change your mind after this one," Ray said.

"Why?"

"You're in love this time. She'll smile at you and ask you to pass the stuffing and you'll be sure you're having the time of your life."

"I'm not in love." It sounded weak to his own ears; he didn't know how he expected Ray to believe him.

"You don't sound very convinced," Ray chuckled. "Cheer up. They'll need us to help lift that bird into the oven."

Ray was right, Nick realized, as the afternoon changed to evening and they'd fed two tired and grateful women hot pepperoni pizza on paper plates. Ray's delivery had arrived, the boxes of Sandetti Specialties scoring a very big hit with the women. Nick decided to look on the bright side. He'd have a chance to see how his products would be received in the Midwest when he tested them on twenty hungry Nebraskans tomorrow.

SARAH WATCHED HIM, careful to make certain he wouldn't know it. Of course he wore the perfect clothes, dark brown slacks and a rust sweater, with a white shirt collar and paisley tie peeking above the neckline. He always looked so put-together and coordinated. She didn't know how he did it.

And of course, he charmed her Great-aunt Esther right away. And Aunt Mary Anne, too, although she raised her gray eyebrows when she saw Ray standing in the living room. "A ghost from the past," the woman had muttered, before enveloping Ray in a hug. "Janet told me you'd come back, but I guess I had to see it with my own eyes. It's been a long time. Since 1945, my goodness!"

"Too long," Ray answered.

Nick and Sarah exchanged a quick glance before Mary Anne's grandchildren rushed in. He'd moved his few possessions down to Ray's room so the children could have the third floor as their playroom, which was something they looked forward to every year. Someone always set up the electric race-car set and Sarah dragged out every toy and game she owned. It was a great escape for the kids to get away from their parents when they felt the need for some privacy.

"Wake up, girl," Mary Anne ordered. "Janet needs you in the kitchen and you're standing here watching the men."

Sarah shook her head. "It's more fun out here."

"I can see why. Having two handsome men in your house sure livens the place up."

"Yes, it does. Aunt Janet seems very happy."

It was Mary Anne's turn to look sad. "She should. She deserves it, after all."

"What do you mean, Aunt Mary?"

The older woman shook her head. "That was long ago, Sarah. And none of our business then—or now, either. I only wish your mother—"

"Wish what?" Sarah hoped she'd answer.

"Never mind. We're ready to put the food out. Think we can all squeeze into the kitchen for grace?"

"We always do, don't we?"

"Yes, we do." Sarah took one last look at the dining room table, stretched to its full length and supplemented with card tables at one end so it reached into the foyer. White linen and an assortment of antique china plates gave it a formal-festive air. "I'll tell everyone to get ready."

"If you can drag Amos away from the dilly dip, it will be a miracle."

"I'll do my best," Sarah promised, heading toward the noisy living room. The television broadcast a pro-football game, which provided background noise. The room was filled with McGrath-Beck relatives, including her seventy-nine-year-old uncle Amos, who was seated beside Nick on the couch. Amos was talking and Nick was listening, and Sarah smiled to herself. Uncle Amos was probably talking about ranching.

She'd been curious about his reaction to her family. Wondered how he'd fit in, wondered if he'd enjoy himself. He was a mystery to her, and yet he was sexy, kind and passionate. Very, very passionate.

She'd told herself to stay away from him, and yet she really didn't want to. Not at all. She wanted to spend the whole day with him and enjoy every minute. That kiss had been incredible, something so out of her realm of experience that she didn't know how to describe it—or fit it into her life. Maybe the men east of the Mississippi kissed like that. An intriguing thought.

But as intrigued as she was by him, there was no reason for her to think that this could go anywhere. He had his life in Rhode Island and she had hers in North Platte. There didn't seem to be any middle ground. It wasn't as if he lived in town or even in the state.

Even though she wished he did. She approached the couch and leaned close to Uncle Amos. "I'm getting everyone together for dinner now. What have you two been talking about?"

Nick smiled. "Pheasant hunting. He thinks I should try it."

Amos nodded. "I can still bring home dinner with the best of 'em."

"I'll just bet you can." Sarah straightened. "Want to spread the word that dinner is ready and we're gathering in the kitchen?"

Nick stood up. "Sure."

"I'm going upstairs to round up the kids."

"I'll go with you," he offered, following her out of the room and into the hallway.

"You don't have—" But he cut off her words with a quick kiss when she turned to protest. Kissing Nick always left her surprised and wanting more. Which, she decided, was exactly his intention. "Don't do that."

"Why not?"

"Someone could see. Then everyone would be talking about it and wondering if there's a big romance going on and I'd spend the rest of the day answering questions out in the kitchen."

"What kind of questions?"

She saw the glimmer of laughter in his eyes and refused to be teased. "Never mind," she said, and started up the wide staircase.

"How many relatives do you have, anyway?"

"This is just a small portion. They—my mother's family—have a reunion every July and at least a hundred people show up."

At the top of the second-floor landing, Sarah peeked into the room Janet used as a sewing room in the wintertime and told the three boys watching *Lethal Weapon III* to turn it off and head for the kitchen. The hungry boys didn't need to be told twice. Then she and Nick rounded up the rest of the children from the third floor and herded them downstairs.

"I know you don't like Thanksgiving," Sarah said as they walked through the dining room. "But I hope you'll enjoy today. It gets a little wild, but—"

He put his finger over her lips. "You don't have to explain your family to me," he said. "If I didn't want to stay I would have gotten on a plane and headed back to Providence."

She shook her head. "No, you wouldn't. Not without Ray."

"One of these days I'm going to have to."

"Yes, well, I guess your vacation has to end some time, doesn't it?"

"Yeah," he said, following her into the crowded kitchen. "I'm afraid it does."

That was the worst part, Sarah decided. Ten days wasn't long enough to get to know someone, and there seemed to be more and more reasons to want to know Nick Ciminero. She told herself to back off, but the worst part was that she liked him so much.

"Time for the blessing," Janet said as the crowd of people grew quiet. "Esther, would you?"

Aunt Esther was more than happy to, and then dinner was served, buffet style, from the large kitchen table. When Sarah carried her plate into the dining room she discovered Nick had saved her a seat. He pointed to the chair next to his. "For you. I've fought off two uncles to keep it empty."

"Thanks." Sarah put her plate down and slid into the empty seat. "But I'll bet my uncles didn't put up much of a fight."

"You're right. They winked and moved on."

"Without saying anything?"

Nick grinned and speared a piece of chestnut stuffing. "Not exactly. Amos told me to watch out or I'd be staying in Nebraska permanently."

It was Sarah's turn to smile. She put her napkin in her lap and picked up her fork. "I don't think you'd want to wear Cornhusker sweatshirts for the rest of your life."

"No, but—"

She didn't get to hear the rest because Janet requested the cranberry sauce and then Esther asked for the saltshaker. Someone passed a basket of rolls around the table and the conversation turned to the Orange Bowl and Nebraska's chances of victory on New Year's Day. Sarah watched Janet, always the gracious hostess, flirting with Ray as she sat at the head of the table. They looked as if they had always been together, and Sarah wished she could somehow turn the clock back to 1945 and solve the mystery of what had obviously been a special kind of love affair.

"PORK AND BEANS!"

"Right!" Esther cried, stopping the game.

Nick peered at the drawing Sarah had made. The tail of a pig was obvious; the pile of beans wasn't. "They're beating us," he told Sarah.

"Everyone's beating us." She pushed the pencil and pad to him.

He picked up the pencil and grimaced. "Pictionary may not be my game. This is pretty cutthroat competition."

She watched as Esther and Amos played the next round. "Not as bad as the football game."

Nick couldn't argue. The younger members of the family had taken sides and played a wild, no-rules touch-football game in the backyard. The snow didn't bother them at all. The only thing that stopped them was the threat of frostbite.

He hadn't expected to have such a good time. Despite the frigid football game—and his team's five-year-

old quarterback—he'd had more fun than he could remember. It had been a long time since he'd experienced
the rowdy enthusiasm of a family holiday. There was
no way to explain to Sarah his childhood holidays with
Rosa and her brood, holidays centered around many
courses of food and wine and laughter. And then the
inevitable letdown of returning to St. Al's.

He'd grown used to it. But, Nick wondered as he
looked around the table, had he grown too used to it?
Was he content to be the outsider, comfortable with returning to nothing? And now, was it too late to change?

"The card," Sarah prompted. "They lost, it's our
turn."

Nick took the card from Amos and read the word in
the brown rectangle. *Alone.* He knew how it felt, but
he sure as hell didn't know how to draw it. He passed
it to the next team and picked up the pencil. Someone
yelled, "Go!"

The stick figure stood apart from the other stick fig-
ures, a frown on his face. "Angry," Sarah tried. Nick
shook his head and pointed to the distance between the
lone figure and the crowd.

"Apart? Left behind? Outside?" Sarah looked back
at Nick who shook his head and pointed the pencil to
the lone figure. And then he pointed to himself and
shrugged slightly. "Alone!"

"Got it," Nick shouted. "She said 'alone'!"

"We're on a roll now," she said, reaching for the die.
"If we can get this next one, we'll start catching up."

"Your turn to draw," Nick said, as Esther slid the box
of cards toward them again.

"Yes, I know." She shot him a questioning look. "The
last one was easy."

"Easy?" Ray asked. "Janet thought I'd drawn a fisherman."

"I guess Nick and I were on the same wavelength," Sarah said, examining the playing card.

"You don't say," Esther drawled. "I would never have guessed."

"Quiet, Esther," Janet told her aunt. "Leave the child alone."

Sarah ignored both of them. "This one is just for us," she told the other players. Sarah picked up her pencil and positioned the pad so Nick could see. "It's green. Are you ready?"

"Ready," he said, and knew he wasn't talking only about the Pictionary game. Someone yelled, "Go," and Nick forced himself to concentrate on the drawing Sarah hurried to complete. "Dog, cat, mouse, lion, tiger—" She stopped and smiled at him.

"Tiger? Is that it?"

"Right!" The rest of the players groaned.

Sarah handed him the die. "Roll a six."

He did. And watched her smile throughout the rest of the game. They came in a respectable third place.

"Anyone for Jeopardy?"

Sarah shook her head. "Not me. I'm going to find a piece of pumpkin pie."

"Me, too." Nick stood up and an eleven-year-old boy took his seat.

"Pumpkin or apple?"

If he thought he'd have privacy in the kitchen, he was very mistaken. Another group was gathered at one end of the table playing cards. He consoled himself with an extra spoonful of whipped cream on top of his pie, then poured two cups of coffee. He didn't know if there was anyplace in this enormous house that held privacy, but he was determined to find it if it existed.

Sarah read his mind. "I don't think you're going to find a quiet place."

"I'm going to try."

She shook her head. "Everyone in the living room is watching football. The kids are upstairs—on both floors. Someone's in the den taking a nap. That just leaves the sun porch, which would have to be about thirty degrees."

"We could wear coats."

"We?"

"We," he confirmed. "I've decided I don't want to let you out of my sight."

She looked surprised. "Why not?"

"Ray has deserted me. You're the only friend I have in this place."

"Oh, come on." She opened the kitchen door. "I'm going to take you to the porch and you'll realize you're better off watching football."

He doubted it. He wanted her alone.

Alone. That Pictionary word was beginning to bother him.

"GO TO BED," Sarah ordered. "I'll take care of the rest."

Janet smiled, but her expression was one of exhaustion. "It was a fun day, wasn't it?"

"The best yet," Sarah said, and realized she meant it. She'd enjoyed the family holiday more than she ever had since she was a child. "But it's over and you need some rest."

"Well, I'm not going to argue." She put the checked dish towel on the counter. "I guess I'm smart enough to know when I've had enough. The men are watching football. I don't think they'll miss me."

"Go on," Sarah urged, concerned about the pallor of Janet's skin. "It's after nine. Way past your bed-time."

Janet patted her face. "Don't work too hard. It will still be here in the morning."

"Don't worry about a thing. Just go to bed."

When Janet left, Sarah realized she was finally alone. But she didn't mind. She turned on the radio to her favorite station and adjusted the volume. There wasn't much left to clean up, just the dessert plates, coffee cups, and odds and ends from bowls and trays. There was probably more in the living room, but she wasn't going to bother now. She didn't have the energy.

Now all she wanted was a turkey sandwich, cold dressing and maybe another piece of pie. Or a few of those cookies from Rhode Island, the ones with the pink glaze on top. Humming along with a Kathy Mattea song, Sarah opened the refrigerator and rummaged through the plastic containers until she found the stuffing and a jar of mayonnaise. She turned, put them on the counter and grabbed a cookie.

"Sarah? I just wanted to—" Nick stopped. "I'm glad you like the cookies."

Sarah swallowed and put the rest of the cookie on the counter. "I think they're addictive."

"That would be good for business." He hesitated, as if he was uncertain about intruding. "I came to say good-night. And thank you for including me today."

Why was he acting so formal? Sarah gestured toward the turkey carcass. "Want a sandwich? I'm fixing myself a little snack."

He smiled and came closer. "I'd like that."

"What about Ray? Do you think he's hungry, too?"

"I sent him to bed. He was dozing off in the chair."

Sarah smiled. "I sent Janet upstairs a few minutes ago. She was determined to clean up the whole house and yet she couldn't stop yawning."

Nick picked up a knife and started slicing the turkey. "They're two of a kind, aren't they?"

"Why would you say that?"

He put down the knife and transferred the slices of white meat to a paper plate. "You don't think they're alike?"

She pushed the mayonnaise jar toward him. "No. Not really."

"Maybe you don't want to see it."

"Why would you say that?"

"You don't want to see that the two of them are in love with each other. I don't know what your reasons are, but I can guess."

Sarah put down the loaf of bread and looked at him. "Oh, really?"

He ignored the sarcasm. "I don't blame you for not wanting to share her—"

"That's not it at all," Sarah interrupted. "I don't want her to get hurt!"

"Don't you think it's romantic, the two of them finding each other again after all these years?"

"Romantic? No," she lied. He was right, but she didn't want to think about Janet being in love with Ray. What would happen when he returned to Rhode Island? Just because it was romantic didn't guarantee a happy ending.

"He loves her," Nick countered.

"He broke her heart years ago."

"You don't know that, Sarah. Maybe it was the other way around. Maybe she dumped him when he came home from the war. After all, he stayed single. She was the one who married."

"You know her. How could she hurt anyone?"

Nick shrugged. "I—*we* may never know what happened in 1945, but I can see what's happening now." He paused to peel another paper plate from the stack in front of him. "And I'm not just talking about Ray and Janet."

Sarah didn't want to hear it. She handed him the bag of snowflake rolls. "What's happening now is you and I are having a late supper. That's it."

He shook his head. His slow smile threatened her ability to breathe. "Wrong, honey."

Honey? She shoved Janet's favorite casserole dish toward him. "Here, have some stuffing."

"Are we going to sit down or should we argue here?"

"Sit," she answered, "after I get something to drink." She opened the refrigerator again. "Diet Coke or, uh, Diet Coke? Guess the kids drank all the root beer."

"Diet Coke."

"Good decision." She pulled two cans from the door and kicked it shut. "You Italian guys are really smart."

"Yeah," he agreed, taking the cold can out of her hand. "And we know a beautiful woman when we see one."

"And you know how to flirt."

"Of course. It's in our blood." He winked at her and she ignored him as she sat down at the table.

Sarah munched potato chips and answered Nick's questions about her various relatives. Nick told her more about his latest trip to Denver. By the time she'd finished her sandwich and eaten three more cookies,

Sarah thought she'd effectively steered the conversation into safe territory, away from Janet and Ray and away from anything personal between Nick and herself.

Because that was the way it should be, the best way to make certain she stayed out of Nick's arms.

8

"I'VE DECIDED that kissing you outside yesterday was probably the stupidest thing I have ever done," Nick announced, pushing his empty plate away.

"Thank you. That's really good for my ego." She reached for another cookie.

"That's not what I meant." He smiled once again and took her hand in his. Her skin was warm. "It cost me a night's sleep."

"You expect me to feel sorry for you?"

"Guess not." He realized that if she'd lost some sleep herself she would never admit it. Especially to him.

She pushed the platter of cookies toward him. "Here. Have some of these."

Nick shook his head and stood up, pulling Sarah to her feet. He took her into his arms and held their clasped hands tight against her hip. Releasing her meant an end to the evening and he would do anything in his power to prevent that from happening. He didn't know how much longer this time would last and he'd learned a long time ago to take what warmth and happiness could be found in the present, because the past didn't exist and the future was just a blank wall. A frightening blank wall on which anything could be written. "No more cookies," he murmured. "Only you."

He lowered his head and touched his lips to hers. She was warm and sweet, like frosting on his lips. Strange, to taste a trace of Rhode Island on this Nebraska woman.

"Nick," she began. He lifted his mouth a fraction of an inch to touch his tongue to the trace of pink sugar on the corner of her mouth.

"What?"

Her hands slid to his shoulders instead of pushing him away. "I thought you said this was stupid."

"Uh-huh," he agreed, trailing kisses along her jaw. The barest trace of perfume lingered near her earlobe. "Stupid to stop."

"Stupid to start."

"No," he countered, looking down into her hazel eyes. There was tenderness there, yes, but a touch of apprehension, too. He could drown in those eyes and die a happy man. "All of a sudden I feel very, very smart."

This time there were no snowflakes to distract him, no opening door or relatives or frigid north wind from the South Dakota plains. This time there was only the two of them, wrapped in each other's arms while the rest of the house slept in contented peace. He made love to her mouth when she parted her lips, and wondered if his hardened body could withstand such pleasure. She was soft and warm and willing in his arms, and Nick moved his hands to her waist to push the cotton sweater aside. He ran his palms along smooth heated skin, up to the texture of lacy bra, and cupped one soft breast in his palm. She moaned against his mouth as his thumb brushed the pointed nub of her breast, and Nick longed to replace his hand with his mouth.

He longed to do so many things.

If he had the time. And as much as he longed to take her with his hard body and his searching hands, he knew if he did he would be irrevocably and irretrievably lost. Forever. And he didn't think he was ready for that. So Nick lifted his mouth from hers, dropped his hand, tugged her sweater into place and, with more regret than he'd ever felt before, stepped away from Sarah's enticing body.

She looked up at him, obviously bewildered and maybe just a little bit relieved. "Is it my turn to feel stupid?"

"No. Sex on the kitchen table may work in the movies, but it's not my style." *And neither is taking advantage of sweet-natured women.*

"I see," she said, backing away a few inches. She reached for the plates on the table, as if clearing the dishes would give her something to do. "Well," she said, trying for lightness, "I don't have a lot of experience in kitchen sex myself, but I'm glad we stopped. I don't usually—"

"What?"

"Nothing." She shrugged and turned away. She wouldn't tell him how he affected her. She was certain a man like Nick had had more women than he could remember. And he would never know that he was only the second man who had touched her breasts and made her knees weak and made her wish that dreams came true.

"I'm leaving in the morning."

She turned to see if he was teasing or serious. Nothing in his eyes showed her any clue to his feelings. "I see."

"Sarah," he began, but she turned away and heard his voice from behind her as she dumped the plates in the trash and opened the refrigerator to put away the leftovers. He handed her a casserole dish. "Let me help," he said.

"I've got it," she replied. "Does Ray know you're leaving?"

"Not yet."

"Then he's not going with you?"

"I don't know."

"If he and Janet are in love, then why would he leave?"

"He wouldn't. But I don't think he'll turn his back on everything he's spent his life working for, not now. It's too important to him."

"I hope you're right, for her sake," Sarah said. Later, after Nick had said good-night and left her alone in the kitchen, she looked out the window and saw that the snow had started falling again. Nick might think he'd be leaving tomorrow, but he could be in for a surprise. She guessed the decision to leave was a sudden one, which meant that maybe—just maybe—kissing her hadn't left him as unaffected as she'd assumed. Simple seduction wouldn't warrant stopping the kiss and starting packing. Unless he'd grown tired of the game.

Sarah knew she had to be very, very careful. She could easily fall in love with Nicholas Ciminero. And falling in love with Nicholas Ciminero could only lead to guaranteed heartache. Did she really want to open herself up for that kind of pain?

In the peace of her room, Sarah opened her desk drawer and looked at the baby's picture. "Happy Thanksgiving," she whispered. "Wherever you are."

"YOU'RE NOT GOING anywhere."

Nick zipped the top of his black leather satchel. "Yes I am."

"Have you looked outside, son?" Ray motioned toward the bedroom window. "It's still snowing. We're in the Midwest, land of blizzards and freezing cattle. Have you called the airport to see if any flights are leaving this morning?"

"No. I thought I'd get a cab and see what's going on when I get there."

"I'll save you a trip. The flights are canceled. I called."

Nick stopped shoving papers into his briefcase and frowned. "You did?"

"Yeah," Ray said, trying to hide his pleasure. "I had to book a flight to—"

"You're going home?"

"No. I booked a flight to Denver for the four of us next Friday afternoon. Thought it was time we took that ski trip I promised you."

"Well, that's real nice of you, Ray, but I'm going back to work."

"You can't go back to work. I've fired you."

Nick closed his briefcase and stared across the room at the old man. "What did you say?"

Ray grinned. He couldn't help it. "I've fired you. Or, if you prefer, you've been laid off. Until after the first of the year."

Nick swore. "You don't mean this."

"I'll make it official if you want to collect unemployment. Actually, I thought I'd just give you a bigger Christmas bonus to cover the extra weeks."

"Cut the crap, Ray. I'm heading back to Providence and back to the office."

Ray shrugged. "Waste your time, then. I'll call the boys and tell them you no longer work for me."

"Why are you doing this?"

"I don't want you to turn into me."

Nick shook his head. "There's no chance of that, old man. I'm not half the man you are."

"True, but you've fallen in love and you're running away. That's a big mistake."

Nick knew Ray spoke the truth. He knew the old man was right, and yet he wanted to run. Run all the way out of town to the airport and fly east to safety. He wanted to be back behind his desk, with his secretary and telephone and fax machine and computer.

And at five o'clock he wanted to come home and find Sarah there.

Accepting defeat, he looked back at Ray. "Guess if I'm unemployed I may as well try being a ski bum. When did you say we were leaving?"

"WE'RE GOING to have to get involved."

"With what?" Janet padded across the kitchen in her pink robe, no longer self-conscious during her quiet breakfasts with Raymond.

"With Sarah and Nick. They can't see what's right in front of their noses."

Janet poured her second cup of coffee and then sat down across the table from Ray. "Oh, I don't think—"

"So I fired him," Ray stated with more than a little satisfaction in his voice.

Janet's hand paused in midair and one drop of coffee slid down the side of the mug. "You didn't!"

"I most certainly did." His eyes twinkled. "You should have seen the look on his face."

"Ray," Janet chided, wondering if he'd gone too far. "How could you do that?"

"It was easy. And don't look at me like that. I've fired people before, woman."

"Not someone who's like a son to you."

Ray didn't look the least bit guilty. "He's merely 'laid off' until the first of the year."

"But how did he take it? He's not going to leave, is he?"

"Not yet. I brought up the ski trip."

"I told you, I'm too old to ski."

He didn't act as if he heard her. "I'm booking four rooms at some place called Copper Mountain, west of Denver. We'll have privacy." He winked at her. "And we won't have to ski."

"Ray," she began, wondering what else this man had in mind besides seeing the Rockies.

"Don't try to talk me out of it. I'm going to seduce you in Colorado or die trying."

She could never tell whether or not he was teasing, so she tried to change the subject. "How are we supposed to get involved with Sarah and Nick? I don't think either one of them would appreciate our meddling."

"Don't worry," he said, leaning back in his chair. "I'll think of something. If we work it right, Jan, we could almost be related."

Janet took another sip of her coffee. She didn't want to be related to Ray. She wanted to turn the clock back to 1945. She wanted to stop the train. She wanted to be young again, but all those things were impossible.

She looked back at Ray, so satisfied with himself. Life was full of impossible things, with the union of Nick and Sarah right up there on top of the list. Somehow she knew Ray would think of something to bring them together.

"HERE, GIVE ME THE SHOVEL."

"No."

Sarah pushed her hair out of her eyes and only suc-
ceeded in getting snow on her face. Her mittens were
wet and her face was already frozen. "Give it to me.
You're going to kill yourself."

"No."

"Fine. Break a leg, then." Men were the most stubborn creatures on the planet. Sarah watched Nick,
bundled in a fashionable ski outfit and gloves bor-
rowed from Fin, struggle to shovel snow off the ice.
Parts of nearby Lake Mahoney had finally frozen,
leaving Betty able to have her annual ice-skating party
at her cabin. Sarah had never dreamed Nick would
want to go along with her, but somehow Janet and Ray
had insisted and it would have been rude to refuse.

"I need the exercise," he insisted, his words muffled
by the thick scarf wrapped around his neck.

She couldn't argue with that, not after having spent
a very long Friday cooped up in the house as the temperature outside hit five degrees, and the windchill
factor plummeted to something way below zero. Embarrassed by her reaction to his kisses, she'd tried to
avoid him as best as she could. There were papers to
correct, lessons to plan and changes in the script for *A
Christmas Carol* to complete. There was plenty to keep
her busy in her room, while the others watched college
football on television and finished the leftovers. When
Betty had called to announce an ice-skating party,
Sarah had been happy to accept the invitation.

Betty called, "The chili's hot, if anyone's interested!"

Nick looked up. "Chili?"

"She's famous for her chili," Sarah informed him,
wondering why he'd wanted to come with her today.

He hadn't said much in the car, even though it was at least a fifteen-minute drive out of town. If they hadn't stopped to pick up Fin, there probably wouldn't have been conversation at all.

Even the various children had the sense to head for shore and remove their skates, regardless of Nick's efforts to enlarge the area of ice available.

"Do you do this often?" He hurried to keep up with her skating strides, his booted feet tenuous on the gray ice.

"Betty and her ex-husband divide up the use of the cabin. She gets it every other month, so we try to get out here once in a while, as long as it's not too cold."

"How do you tell?"

It was a rhetorical question. Sarah tried to hide her laughter, but it was no use. She looked up at Nick as she sat down on the frozen shoreline. "You don't."

He grinned back. "That's what I thought. You Nebraskans take the weather in stride, I'll say that for you."

"You look like you're surviving."

He crouched in front of her and pushed her hands away from her skate lace. He removed his gloves and took over the job himself. "Thanks to Fin's army boots."

It was an oddly intimate arrangement, sitting on the frozen grass and feeling Nick's strong fingers on her skates. He took his time, especially when he rubbed warmth into her feet before handing her boots to her. "Thanks," was about all she could manage. If it felt that good just having him undress her feet, what could he do to the rest of her?

It was a frightening question, and Sarah hurried to shove her feet into her frigid boots. Nick helped her up and kept her hand in his as they climbed the hill to the cabin. Sarah had to admit that all of a sudden she was having a good time.

And it continued throughout the afternoon, with several faculty members and their children either skating, eating chili, helping assemble a jigsaw puzzle or shooting pool on the huge table that took up one section of the one-room cabin. A sleeping loft was reached by a ladder, and a small bathroom was tucked into one corner near the kitchen, but the rest of the room was lined by windows that overlooked the lake and the approaching darkness.

"Do me a favor, Sarah?"

"Sure." She held a glass of wine, almost finished. The warmth of the wine had seeped through her body and finally warmed her blood. Lights began to shine around the lake as people lit the lamps. Everyone else had gone home except Nick and Fin.

"Close up for me?" Betty lowered her voice. "I offered to give Fin a ride home and he invited me to the movies. If we leave now we can make the early show."

Sarah smiled. "Wow. I'm impressed."

"Me, too." Her eyes sparkled in the dim light. "I never thought I had a chance with him."

"He seems like a nice man."

"So's Nick." Betty winked. "Stay as long as you want. There's no need to hurry away. Just put another log on the fire and pour another glass of wine. Make the man forget where Rhode Island is."

"I don't think there's much chance of that."

"We'll see." Betty grabbed her coat and went over to Nick, who stood by the pool table talking with Fin. The men looked relaxed, with the pool cues in their hands.

Nick fit right in, which finally ceased to surprise her. He even talked Betty into sharing her chili recipe with him.

"Don't forget," Betty said, "you're going to give me the recipe for the meatballs."

"I promise."

"With complete directions."

"Of course. In detail."

Sarah waved goodbye and suddenly they were alone again. She didn't have a chance, no matter what she did. If she took him to a party with twenty people, she'd end up alone with him—and even worse, alone with him in an intimate cabin complete with fireplace, wine and three cushy sofas.

Nick motioned toward the pool table. "Do you play?"

"About as well as you ice-skate."

He parked the cue in the holder on the wall. The only sound was Betty's Volvo roaring to life, and then in a moment it was quiet again.

"I told Betty we'd lock up." Then, so he wouldn't think she'd engineered their being alone together, she added, "She was in a hurry. Fin asked her to the movies and they wanted to make the early show."

"Yes," Nick said. "He told me."

"He did?"

Nick nodded. "He likes her."

"I'm glad."

"I thought you might have been involved with him when I first met him."

Sarah smiled. "No. We barely know each other."

"That's another one of the things I don't understand about you."

"What is?"

"The fact that you have no involvements, no men calling."

"I like it that way," she answered, and finished her glass of wine. "Maybe we should start getting home."

He ignored her words and went over to the table and picked up the half-empty wine bottle. Then he joined her on the couch and refilled her glass. "Why do you like it that way?"

"It's easier."

"Meaning, it's safer."

"Right."

"Okay," he agreed. "I'll buy that. But what happens when you meet someone and you decide it's not worth it to be safe anymore, that maybe, just maybe, you *have* to take the risk."

"That hasn't happened yet."

He looked at her for a long moment. "Never?"

Sarah didn't know what to say, but she knew the truth wasn't going to be one of her options. She couldn't blurt out, *It's happening to me, too, every time you touch me, every time you walk into a room and look at me and smile.* Besides, he might not be talking about her—them—at all.

She played with her wineglass, slowly twirling the delicate stem between her fingers until Nick plucked it from her hand and set it on the table beside him. "Seems a shame to waste a perfectly good fire," he said, sliding closer. He put his arm around her and leaned her head against his shoulder. "There," he declared. "This is much better."

She couldn't argue. Snuggling with a man on a cold November night wasn't half bad, especially in front of a crackling fire in an isolated cabin.

"We could make love on this couch," he said.

"Yes, we could," Sarah agreed, tempted beyond all reason. "But we're not going to."

"Are you sure?" He sounded as if he was trying not to laugh, so Sarah twisted around to look at him. "I hate to waste a good fire."

"Quit joking," she said and smiled in spite of herself.

"Who's joking? Come here," he said, and lifted her onto his lap so that she faced him. "Put your arms around my neck," he instructed.

"That's safe enough." She didn't feel safe at all, not with his hard thighs under her. Still, it was so tempting to snuggle with Nick in total privacy.

His eyebrows rose. "Give me some time. That's only the first step."

She put her arms around his neck and felt the soft hair underneath her fingertips. "I've heard about men like you."

"Yeah, we Italian guys are real dangerous in Nebraska."

"That's what I've heard."

"What else have you heard?"

She looked down into those gorgeous brown eyes and suddenly she didn't feel like being silly any longer. "I've heard that it's foolish to fall for a man who isn't going to be around next week or next month or next year. That it's dangerous to trust someone you've only known for ten days."

"Eleven days, counting today."

"What's the difference?"

"I need all the help I can get," he teased, running his hand up her arm. "By the way, this is a very thick sweater."

"This is a very cold state."

"It's hard to feel you."

"Good," she laughed, but when she looked at him her arms tightened around his neck and he pulled her toward him. This time she knew the taste of him, knew the feel of his lips on hers, recognized the fresh scent of his after-shave and the texture of his bottom lip. It didn't matter that she wore thick jeans and underneath, long underwear. Her senses still rioted as his hands caressed her back and held her against him.

She felt as if she couldn't get close enough. Despite the layers of clothing between them, she could feel his arousal, feel how much he wanted her. Could feel the control he exerted.

Her fingers moved to his shoulders, his hands slid up her sweater, pulled the silk camisole from the waistband of her jeans and finally caressed her bare back.

It was heaven, she decided, as his hands moved to her breasts. Heaven to kiss and touch and feel once again. She shoved all sensible thoughts aside as his fingertips caressed her and sent waves of sweet warmth rippling along her skin. He moved lower to the snap on her waistband and tugged at the zipper of her jeans. He slipped one hand inside and slid his palm over the long underwear. His hand stilled, and he chuckled against her mouth.

"How many layers of clothing do you have on?" he asked, taking his mouth from hers and smiling down into her eyes.

"I get cold."

His hands moved to her waist. "You don't feel cold."

"No. Right now I'm not cold at all. That's the problem." She attempted to move away from him, but his hands tightened around her waist.

"Don't," he ordered, and Sarah looked up at him once again. She saw only passion and tenderness in his eyes, and she stopped her attempt to leave.

"This isn't a good idea," she whispered. "I may be attracted to you, I may even like you a lot, but I can't make love to you."

He moved his hands lower, to probe the elastic around her waist. His fingers dipped beneath the underwear and caressed her bare skin. "No?"

Sarah smiled, hoping he didn't notice the tiny shivers she tried with no success to hide. "No."

She moved away from him, and this time he let her go. She reminded herself that it was the best decision, despite the aching in her body that would bother her for hours. She was in great danger of falling in love with him. Making love would be the biggest mistake she could make. If she'd learned one thing in twenty-seven years, it was that. She'd just have to try harder to harden her heart.

"At least you admitted you may like me." He smiled, and those brown eyes seemed to see all of her secrets. "We're making progress."

"WE'RE DOING WHAT?"

"Going skiing," Janet answered. "Would you hand me that cookie sheet?"

Sarah reached over and slid the pan toward her aunt. Janet was never happier than when she was baking, so the prospect of Christmas cookies sent her into ecstasy. "Aunt Janet, have you ever been skiing?"

"No, but I can take lessons."

"Have you talked to your doctor about this?"

"No, but if it makes you feel better, I will. I can enjoy the scenery. I haven't been up to the mountains in years, not since before Jim died."

"Neither have I, but—"

"Then we'll all have a terrific time."

"I can't afford—"

"It's Ray's treat, his way of thanking us for the hospitality, so don't worry."

Don't worry? Impossible. Sarah watched Janet carefully transfer tree-shaped cookies onto the baking sheet. "Why are you making cookies? It's not even December yet."

"I'll freeze most of them. Besides, if I do a little at a time it's not so tiring when Christmas comes."

Sarah eyed the huge bowl of cookie dough. It didn't look like Janet was making a little bit at a time. "You need to slow down, remember?"

"I'm fine. You don't need to spend one teaspoon of energy worrying about your old aunt. I can take care of myself, you know."

Sarah remembered what the cardiologist said during their last visit and bit back a retort. It would do no good to remind her aunt. Ray's arrival had changed everything, and now they were going *skiing?*

"I can't believe I'm hearing this," she said, taking her usual seat on the stool and leaning on the counter.

"Can't believe what?" Ray asked, bouncing into the room. His cheeks were glowing, and his eyes twinkled as he looked back and forth between the two women.

"The ski trip, Ray. I don't think I can—"

"Sure you can!" he interrupted. "We'll leave on Friday, at whatever time is convenient for you. I had planned to fly, but Janet wanted to drive if the weather was good. What do you think?"

"I—"

But it was Janet's turn to interrupt. "She thinks it sounds wonderful," she told him, with a warning glance at Sarah. "We'll have a lovely time."

"What about Nick? What does he think of all this?"

Ray grinned. "He likes to ski."

"I thought he was anxious to get back to work."

Ray stepped closer and peered into the bowl. "I fired him."

"You what?"

"Fired him." When Janet turned her back to put the pan of cookies into the oven he dipped his finger into the dough and sampled it. Then he winked at Sarah. "How was school today? That play of yours coming along all right?"

Sarah allowed Ray to change the subject. "Tiny Tim can't remember his lines and the Ghost of Christmas Future is going to Disneyworld."

"Lucky ghost."

"Not for me. She's leaving the night before the play, so one of the other girls is learning the lines."

"Sounds like our little trip to Denver will be a good break for you."

"Speaking of that, where's Nick?" She'd like to hear his reaction to their "little trip."

Janet adjusted the timer and wiped her hands on her apron. "I sent him to the store for powdered sugar. He didn't seem to mind."

Ray nodded. "He loves it. My sister taught him how to cook because he was always hanging around the kitchen talking to her. So she put him to work." Ray chuckled. "He didn't mind at all, because it gave him an excuse to be with her."

"Did he live next door?"

Ray looked surprised. "He didn't tell you?" Sarah shook her head, so he explained. "Well, he doesn't talk about his past much. He was an orphan, lived at St. Aloysius's. That was a home for boys," he added. "My sister Rosa was one of the cooks there. She started bringing him home with her on weekends and holidays so he became like part of the family." He smiled. "Of course, he looked just like one of us, too."

"But what about his parents?"

Here Ray just shook his head. "Nick doesn't talk about it much, but I guess there was a lot of violence in his life. I don't think he ever knew his father, and from what little he's said, I gather his mother only caused him great pain. He was in St. Al's from the time he was five until he was eighteen and on his own. He put himself through college, and worked for me since he was fourteen."

"How sad," Janet said. "How very, very sad growing up in an institution. I don't know how anyone can get along without family."

"He had the Sandettis," Ray reminded her. "And from the first time I met him I knew he was a kid who was a survivor. He's worked hard to make up for the things he didn't have. It killed him to be different from the other kids, but it made him a very strong man. And a very successful one."

"And your sister?"

"Died eight years ago. Nick and I bought her a condo in Florida so she could spend the winter months in the sun, but she only spent two months there before she died. She had a stroke—high blood pressure. She was very proud of that boy. And she was the closest thing to a mother Nick ever had."

"She must have been a lovely person," Janet said as the bell on the timer rang. She flipped it off and opened the oven door to check the cookies.

"When she died the family just seemed to drift apart, although Nick and I still spend the holidays together."

"Just the two of you?" Janet was obviously shocked. "I always pictured you in the middle of a large family."

"Did you picture me married with five children, too?" he teased.

"Yes," she answered, but her expression was sad. "As a matter of fact, I did."

"Well." He cleared his throat. "I pictured you just like this, standing in a kitchen baking cookies."

As the two of them looked at each other, Sarah's heart stopped beating for a long moment. It was as if she held her breath until the world settled back into place once more.

Ray and Janet had loved each other a long time ago. If they hadn't, why would being together matter so much to them now? Nick had been right about that, and now Sarah realized the truth in that observation. She watched as Janet picked up the rolling pin and Ray filched more cookie dough. She slid off the stool and made an excuse no one heard as she tiptoed out of the room, leaving the two of them alone together, again. Which seemed to be exactly the way they liked it.

9

"I'M SORRY I ever started this," Sarah muttered, leafing through the stack of papers on her desk.

"Started what?"

Sarah looked up to see Betty standing in the doorway. "I was talking to myself. Sorry."

Betty stepped inside the empty classroom. "What, no lunch today?"

"I thought I'd eat here at the desk and catch up on some of this work. I don't seem to be getting as much done at home as I used to."

"Of course not, with the handsome Italian cook living with you."

"Stop teasing."

"No way. It's too much fun." Betty looked over Sarah's shoulder at the papers. "'Family Holiday Traditions'? What's wrong with that?"

"I'm not in the mood this year."

"What's the matter? You usually throw yourself into the Christmas season with a vengeance."

Betty didn't know how accurate she was. The only person who had ever understood was Aunt Janet, and this year there were few moments for any kind of conversation between them. She missed her aunt's company and yet couldn't help but be pleased that Janet was so happy, tooting around the countryside with Ray. "I've been busy at home."

"No kidding."

"How'd the date with Fin go?"

"Wonderfully." Betty smiled once again, as if she couldn't stop herself. "He's a very nice man."

"Yep. He sure seems to be."

"And the kids like him."

"*All* the kids like him."

"And he seems to like me, too."

"Of course he does." Sarah leaned back in her chair. "You're gorgeous, smart and kind. Why wouldn't he like you?"

Betty blushed. "I think we're going out to dinner Friday night. Would you and Nick like to go with us? It'd be fun."

"I'm sure it would." And she meant it, too. "But I'm—we're—going skiing in Denver this weekend."

"Who's *we?*"

"The four of us—including the senior citizens. In fact, it was Ray's idea. Some sort of early Christmas present."

"Wow, I'm impressed."

"Me, too, except..." She stopped, uncertain as to exactly why she hesitated to hop in the car and head west on Interstate 80.

"Except what?" Betty perched on top of a student desk. "From the looks of things at the cabin last weekend, I'd assume that you and Nick Ciminero are getting along well enough to go skiing together. What's going on?"

Sarah just shook her head. "I don't know, Betty. He's a wonderful man, but—"

"What—no chemistry? No physical attraction?"

Sarah shook her head again. "No, I couldn't say that." In fact, the truth was that they could hardly keep their hands off each other.

"What, then? Nothing in common? He hates kids? Is he an ex-con?"

"No." She laughed, despite her resolve to end the conversation. "I guess we come from different worlds, different life-styles. He's just a brief guest in my home, that's all."

"It's not like he's from Siberia, Sarah. He doesn't speak a different language or anything. And even if he did, what difference would it make if you were in love?"

"Who said anything about love?"

Betty sighed. "No one, I guess. But I see the way he looks at you and I see the way you look at him. I don't know what either one of you is thinking, but what you're feeling sure shows."

"I don't want to get hurt." It was the most honest thing she could think to say.

"No one does," her friend said with a gentle smile. "But unless you live in a bubble, you can't help it. It's just part of living."

Sarah wondered if Betty was right. *Just part of living.* And was she living, really living? Or was she going through the motions—nice, safe little motions—all the while protecting herself from any involvement, any pain, any risk?

She thought of Nick's warm brown eyes and sexy mouth and those hands of his that had a certain way of touching her that made her weak. Maybe safety was grossly overrated.

SALLY COMISKI, the Ghost of Christmas Past, raised her voice above the chattering fifth-graders and said, "Come, it's time to see the past and where you've been and what you've done. For now is Christmas Eve, and you must—"

She stopped, and looked helplessly at Sarah. "I can't remember, Miss McGrath!"

Sarah didn't have to look down at the paper in front of her. She lowered her voice and attempted a spooky tone. "For now is Christmas Eve, and you must answer for your actions and see what is to come." She paused. "Okay, Sally. Try it again."

Sally stammered the lines and the bell rang. Sarah almost laughed at the relief on the child's face.

"Okay, everyone. Remember to practice tonight at home. And don't forget the social studies quiz tomorrow!"

As soon as the children left the classroom, Nick walked in. "I've been to the supermarket and I thought you might need a ride home." He shivered. "The windchill is fourteen below."

"What errand did Janet send you on this time? Sugar, flour, vanilla extract?"

"Almonds."

"You're a very patient man."

"Sometimes." The look he gave her was X-rated. "When I think it's worth the wait."

"Give me a minute to get my things, okay?"

"Sure." He looked at the script. "'You must answer for your actions and see what is to come'?" He looked up at Sarah. "Pretty grim stuff."

"Fifth-graders are a little bloodthirsty."

He read more and then put the paper down. "I don't think I want to spend Christmas Eve looking at the past and answering for my mistakes. That sounds too depressing."

"It's not supposed to be depressing. It's supposed to be a learning experience. At least, that's what it was for Scrooge."

"Well, Scrooge deserved it, I suppose. Or Dickens thought he did."

She tried for levity. "Didn't you make any mistakes this year that you want to think about?"

He shook his head. "Sure, I made mistakes. But nothing I want to lose a night's sleep over. Even Scrooge did his best to correct his mistakes and move on, didn't he?"

Sarah put her coat on and opened the desk drawer to remove her purse. "I suppose. Dickens may have made it look too easy."

He looked surprised. "It makes for a good story, though. Poor Scrooge. He was hit over the head with his mistakes, wasn't he? I don't think I'd want to spend a night like he did."

"Neither would I."

"You have ghosts, Sarah?"

"Everyone does." For one ridiculous second she was tempted to tell him about being seventeen and falling in love and giving birth to Jenny. She wondered if he would understand.

"Want to tell me about them?"

"No."

"Then what do you do with your ghosts, Sarah?"

She looked up at him and realized he was serious with his question. It was hard to keep the bitterness out of her voice as she replied, "I try not to think about them."

"Does that work?"

"Most of the time." She took a deep breath. "And what about you? Ray told me you grew up in an orphanage. You must wonder where your family is. It has to cause you pain. Or are you over that part of your life?"

"Sometimes I think about them, sure. And I wonder why they did the things they did, but I've come to the realization that I was probably better off where I was, in St. Al's. At least it was safe." He looked as if he wanted to take her into his arms. "But I faced all those demons a long time ago, and then I moved on. I prefer the Ghost of Christmas Future myself. I like looking ahead."

Of course he would, Sarah realized. That's where his ambition came from.

"And you, Sarah? What do you believe in?" he asked, holding the door open for her as they left the empty classroom. "No, don't tell me, I already know."

"What?"

"The Ghost of Christmas Busy," he replied. "What else?"

Sarah laughed, but she had to admit that Nick was closer to the truth than he knew. Besides, she didn't really believe that people were meant to go poking into the dusty corners of their past. That's what attics were for.

"Sarah," he said, taking her arm and stopping her in the hall. "It takes a lot of energy to keep the ghosts away." He paused, and Sarah wished he'd hold her in his very strong arms and let her lean against him. But he didn't move, just kept his grip on her shoulders as he looked down at her. "If you ever want to face them, you wouldn't have to do it alone."

She didn't even attempt to speak. She looked up into his very handsome, very serious and very kind face and realized she'd made the second biggest mistake of her life: she'd fallen in love with Nicholas Ciminero.

"WE DON'T NEED four rooms. It's a waste of money."

"Maybe."

Janet tried again. "It's not too late to change it."

Ray picked up two suitcases and started down the hallway toward the west wing of the large hotel. "I'm not changing anything," he replied.

"But, Ray—"

He turned around to face her and she almost collided with him. "This is a Christmas present, Peaches. For all of us. We each have our own rooms. You can order from room service, have your clothes pressed, your skis waxed, whatever. It's a gift from me, so *please* stop fretting about it. This weekend is not going to bankrupt me."

Janet turned around to see if Nick and Sarah had overheard, but they were not behind them. "Ray, wait!"

"For what?"

"Nick and Sarah. We lost them."

"No." He smiled his typical charming smile, and Janet's heart skipped a beat. She wondered if she'd remembered her medication.

"No?"

"They have two rooms in the east wing. We're in the west."

"Ray—"

"Don't lecture me. I requested rooms on the first floor and they only had two left. You and me. Let the young people stay on the second story and climb the stairs, all right?"

"All right."

"Besides, those two have been looking at each other for two weeks now."

"I think they've done more than looking," Janet added. "Sarah blushes whenever he looks at her. I never would have believed it unless I'd seen it with my own eyes."

Ray stopped in front of a door and checked the number on the key. He handed the key to Janet. "This one's yours."

Janet inserted the key and the door swung open to reveal a spacious room complete with double bed and sliding glass doors. The drapes were pulled back to reveal ski slopes and snow. Ray set her suitcase on the bed.

"Well? What do you think?"

"I can't believe I'm here."

"Neither can I. I'm glad Nick was driving."

"No, I didn't mean the mountain roads. I meant, here with you after all these years."

"Didn't I promise you a trip to Colorado in one of my letters?"

Janet swallowed hard. He'd left out the word *honeymoon*. Winter or summer, they were to have spent their honeymoon in Colorado. "I remember," she managed to say.

"I try to keep my promises." Ray stepped closer and took her face between his hands. He kissed her lips for a long moment and then lifted his head to look down into her eyes. Janet wondered at the love she saw there, or was this wishful thinking? She would have liked to believe what she saw in his eyes, but she knew that their love had died a long time ago. Some things were best left in the past.

"Believe it, my love," Ray whispered, his words putting an end to all her disbelief. "We're finally going to have a weekend to remember."

Janet didn't know how she made it through dinner, although the roast beef was excellent and the large rustic dining room was decorated for Christmas. Everything had a holiday feeling, but it wouldn't have mattered if the room was dingy and draped in black. It was a special evening because she and Ray were together. Even if it was just for a few days, it didn't matter anymore.

He wanted to make love to her. He'd made it clear, but the thought of having sex was daunting. It had been years. Seven years, actually. Was she too old? Not really, just out of practice. She sipped her coffee without tasting it.

Nick and Sarah seemed content to linger over dessert and coffee, but Ray didn't contribute to the conversation.

"I'm going to turn in early," Ray said finally. "I know you'll excuse me." He stood up and turned to Janet. "What about you, Jan?"

To her surprise, the words tripped out. "It's been a long day," she said, truthfully. "I need some rest, too. We'll leave the young people to discuss skiing. Good night, you two. I'll see you in the morning."

Nick and Sarah stood up, too. "We'll see you in the morning," Sarah said. Janet put her hand in Ray's and allowed him to lead her out of the dining room. They stayed hand in hand as they walked toward the lobby, and Ray's hand tightened around hers as he led her into a dark nightclub.

"One dance," he said.

"Ray," she said, hesitating when she saw the crowds of young people dancing to an energetic country song. "I don't think—"

"Shh," he said, waving to the young woman in front of the microphone. She smiled, her black sequins shimmering under the spotlight, and gave Ray a thumbs-up sign. The song ended on a high note, and when it was over the young woman swept her long blond hair away from her face and stepped closer to the microphone.

"This next song is a special request." She winked at Ray. "A lot of people have recorded it since it was written in 1938, and it's been a song for lovers, especially during World War II." The pianist began the chord progression. "So for all you lovers out there—enjoy. You know who you are."

She nodded to the pianist, and then began to sing "I'll Be Seeing You."

Ray tugged Janet onto the dance floor and took her in his arms. The steps came back to them both, though they'd only danced together in her living room. Fifty years melted away, disappearing into the air like the notes from the song. They danced as if they'd never stopped, and Janet knew she never wanted to leave his arms. The singer seemed to make the song last longer than Janet remembered, which was even better. She had no idea that the crowd of people, intrigued by the older couple, had withdrawn to the sides of the dance floor in order to watch. Her feet followed his every intricate step.

The singer held the last note for a long moment, until there was nothing left but the brief final notes of the piano. Ray stopped, but held Janet for one moment more, as if impressing the feel of her in his arms.

She heard the applause, looked around to see the crowd of people looking at them and clapping their approval. It was embarrassing, but she wouldn't have missed it for anything in the world. She was in Colorado, just like they'd planned. She might not be nineteen anymore, but she was with the man she loved. "Ray—"

He stepped back and kept his arm around her waist as they left the dance floor. When they reached the side, he waved to the singer, then took Janet's hand and led her through the crowd and out the door.

She tried again. She wished she could tell him what hearing that song had meant to her, what wistful memories it recalled. He must have arranged it sometime during dinner. "Ray—"

"What?"

"I'm glad my room isn't too far away."

His grip on her arm tightened. "After waiting fifty years, I'd walk miles."

"You would?"

"After loving you for so long, do you think I'd let anything stop me now?"

Janet smiled to herself and hurried to keep up with his long strides. "We have all night," she reminded him, trying to catch her breath.

He stopped in front of his door and pulled out the key. "We have all *weekend*."

"YOU'RE CRYING."

Sarah wiped the tears from her face, not having realized they were there until he mentioned it. She'd watched two people dance as if they were the only two people in the world. One of those people was her aunt, and the other was a man who up until a few weeks ago had been a stranger.

"You've been right all along," she sniffed, turning to look at Nick. "They loved each other, didn't they?"

"Yes, and I'm sure they still do." He took her arm and steered her toward the bar.

"We shouldn't have followed them in here."

She thought it kind that Nick politely refrained from pointing out that it was her idea, not his. "Would you like something to drink?"

More than anything she could think of right now. "Yes."

"Wine?"

"Yes—no. Something stronger. Brandy, I think."

His eyebrows rose. "All right." He turned to the bartender. "Two brandies."

When he collected the drinks he led her to a tiny round table in the corner. A glass globe protected the flickering candle in the center of the pine top as they sat down on the plain wooden chairs.

Sarah raised her glass. "Well, here's to Colorado."

Nick touched his glass to hers. "I thought you would prefer a more romantic toast."

Sarah took a swallow of the brandy and let the liquid burn her throat before she replied, "I'm not much of a romantic."

She'd been dreading this moment of being alone with Nick. She'd avoided it for days, since she'd realized that she'd fallen in love with a man with whom she had nothing in common. A man who lived fifteen hundred miles away and didn't know anything about gelatin salad or University of Nebraska football.

"You've been avoiding me for days," the man stated in his usual forthright way. "Why?"

She wasn't going to lie. "I thought it was a good idea."

He looked surprised that she didn't deny it. "Why?"

"Every time we're alone together we end up in each other's arms. I don't think that's very smart."

"Why?" he repeated for the third time. "I happen to enjoy kissing you."

"Kissing is one thing. Making love is another. We can't."

"No?"

She shook her head and picked up her glass. "No."

He studied her expression for a long moment. "Sarah, are you a virgin?"

She choked on the mouthful of brandy. When she wiped her mouth, she put down the napkin and managed to say, "No. I'm not."

"But you're attracted to me." Since she didn't deny it, he continued. "And I'm attracted to you. Very attracted."

And I've fallen in love with you. She wondered how fast he'd run if she said the words out loud.

"We're both single, heterosexual and healthy." He paused. "I have never taken risks with sex," he admitted. "And I'm not, never have been, promiscuous." He smiled, the corners of his mouth turning down. "I'm very particular about who I sleep with."

"I appreciate the honesty, but—" She hesitated. It was obviously her turn to say something about her sex life. As if she had one. "It's been years since I've had a, uh, relationship."

"Why?"

Sarah wasn't about to get into that. "I haven't wanted one."

"And now?"

She looked at him, suddenly needing to be honest. "I'm not sure."

"Well, *I* am. I'd like to take your hand and lead you upstairs to my room and make love to you all night long."

Sarah gulped. Unfortunately, it was exactly what she wanted, too, but she couldn't afford another mistake. She couldn't let herself love again. Could she? Sarah looked into Nick's now-familiar face and felt her resolve wavering.

Then he smiled, a lopsided smile that made her heart turn over. "You don't know how you affect me."

"How do you feel about dancing?"

His smile widened. "My body against your body?"

"Yes."

"I'd love it."

"Good. I think we need some exercise." She stood up and reached for his hand. As soon as their hands connected she knew she had to be very careful. And very, very sure of what she wanted.

Nick led her to the dance floor and tucked her into his arms as the band played a soft country tune. "In other words, you're telling me not to rush you."

"I'm telling you I'd like to dance."

He pulled her closer. "That's a start."

She couldn't help snuggling against him as they danced. She luxuriated in the feel of his hard body against hers. She had him all to herself, a surprisingly heady feeling. No one knew them, so they might as well have been alone in the crowded, smoky lounge. She didn't know that dancing was foreplay. If she'd ever known, she'd forgotten. They could have been anybody—newlyweds, an old married couple on a vacation, lovers.... No one in the room knew or cared.

And she could pretend, pretend he was hers forever. Pretend they'd been happy for years and would be in the years to come. Pretend that all the ghosts of other memories, other times, were just vague wisps of air. Pretend that nothing hurtful could touch them. And so she allowed herself to melt into his arms, until the music stopped.

Much later, after the singer finished the last set and the band unplugged their instruments, Nick and Sarah headed down the hall and up the staircase to the second floor. It seemed natural to hold his hand as if they'd been together for years, not weeks.

They stopped in front of her door and Sarah dug through her purse for the key. Nick stopped her when he put his hand on her arm. She looked up at him, and he pulled a key from his pants pocket. "Our rooms connect."

There wasn't any decision, after all. "I saw that."

"In fifteen minutes I'll open my door and you open yours."

She couldn't say a word. He let go of her wrist and she pulled the key out and opened her door. She shut it carefully behind her before expelling the breath she'd been holding.

She looked at her watch. It was 12:31. Fifteen minutes was not a long time to decide whether or not to spend the night with a handsome Italian chef from New England.

He's practically a stranger. Still, she slipped out of her clothes in record time. She'd take a quick shower and think about all the reasons not to make love with Nicholas Ciminero. It was a luxurious and heady thought. By the time she'd showered, toweled off and wrapped herself in a floral terry-cloth robe, she was no closer to talking herself out of an affair, however brief.

You're in love with him. Sex will only complicate an already complicated situation. Sarah dabbed perfume between her breasts and brushed her hair.

He doesn't love you. She picked up her watch from the bathroom counter. Three minutes to go.

She left the bathroom and took a deep breath as she eyed the door between the closet and the dresser. Had he opened his side yet? Or would he wait for her to open her door first?

This was ridiculous. She was a grown woman and yet she was on top of a snow-covered mountain staring at a closed door. Before she could change her mind, she stepped forward, making no sound on the carpet. She slid the bar from the latch and turned the handle, but nothing happened. She tugged harder, but the door didn't budge.

NICK WAITED. He'd unlocked the connecting door as soon as he'd walked into the room, leaving the door wide open as he'd poured himself a drink. He and Ray had brought wine and glasses, which had been Ray's idea. Somehow he'd ended up with the cooler in his room, though. At least he could offer Sarah some wine.

If she ever opened the door, that is. He glanced at his watch. She'd had plenty of time and the damn door was still closed tighter than a clam at low tide.

She'd changed her mind. The gut-wrenching disappointment hit him hard, and he sucked in his breath as the realization washed over him. *She's not coming.* There was more than just a one-night stand at stake. He was falling in love with her, and he didn't know what to do about it.

Although making love to her certainly seemed like a good way to start.

Nick grimaced, looked at his watch again, then finished his wine. And kept staring at the damn door as if he could will it to open by the sheer force of his gaze.

Five minutes later he decided to stop torturing himself. She'd had twenty-five minutes to change her mind, and he might as well accept it. Nick unbuttoned his shirt, kicked off his loafers and headed to the bathroom for a cold shower. It was going to be a long night.

SARAH KNOCKED quietly on the door, then wondered what good it would do. Nick couldn't open it. She thought about going to his room, but going into the corridor dressed in nothing but wraparound terry cloth didn't seem like a good idea. She could call the front desk and have them send someone up to fix the door, but it was one o'clock in the morning. How would she explain wanting to open the door so she and the man next to her could make love?

Besides, what if he'd changed his mind? She was being irrational, she knew, but what if the door wouldn't open because he preferred it that way?

She was no smoldering beauty, not sophisticated or worldly. She was certain he was more accustomed to women like that. Sarah plopped on the bed—her big wide double bed—and sat cross-legged facing the stubbornly resisting door. Her feet were cold, and her palms damp. She took a deep breath and looked at the phone. The simple solution was to call him. If he'd changed his mind, she deserved an explanation.

If not, she'd give him the opportunity to do a manly thing like knock the door down. Sarah lifted the receiver and dialed. She waited while the phone rang seven times. Then she put the receiver back into its cradle and climbed off the bed for the moment it took to turn down the covers, throw on her flannel nightgown and turn off the bedside light.

Nick Ciminero owed her an explanation. Sarah pulled the covers up to her chin and rubbed her cold feet together. It was ironic—for years she'd been celibate, despite a few longings for someone to love, but she'd never believed it would happen to her.

And, she thought wryly, snuggling deeper into her pillow, it still hadn't.

HE SLID into the warm bed, careful not to wake her. Soft, satin skin and the sweet scent of a woman—*his* woman—enveloped him. It was all he could do to not wake her, love her, fit himself inside of her and watch her waken as he made love to her.

Ray made certain the covers were tucked around Janet's shoulder before he eased himself into the bed. They'd made love for a long, long time. And, sixty-seven or nineteen, he couldn't get enough of her.

He touched one full breast, and Janet made a little sound in her sleep. She turned toward him and blinked sleepily.

"Ray?"

"I'm here," he whispered, enjoying the feel of her under his palm.

"I know." She smiled. "I'm glad you didn't leave and go back to your room. Why are you awake?"

"I couldn't sleep. I kept thinking about us, wondering where we went wrong. I didn't know that fate would be so generous, giving me a second chance with you." He didn't know that miracles still happened, didn't really believe that he could go back to the past and erase the mistakes he had made.

Maybe not erase, he decided, but at least atone.

"It's no time for regrets," Janet murmured, sliding closer. "We're past that, and we both have too many reasons to regret what happened. It's time to be grateful for what we have."

"All right," Ray answered, sliding his hand up to her shoulder. "For whatever time we have left together, I promise to be very, very grateful." When she smiled, he reached for her in the darkness and tucked her against his naked body. "Can I be grateful and make love to you at the same time?"

"I think that's a *very* good idea," she answered and, no longer shy, she reached for him in the darkness.

10

"GOOD MORNING, Sarah. Sleep well?"

Sarah turned around to see Nick sitting alone at a table for four. She'd hoped to have a quiet breakfast all alone, but obviously Nick had beaten her to the dining room. He also looked interested in her answer.

"Good morning. And yes, I did." Sarah refused to give him the satisfaction of knowing she had tossed and turned for hours. She had decided, while lying awake in that damn bed, that she would pretend last night never happened. It would be easier that way.

Until now. Nick looked rested, clean-shaven and very much in control. She decided to try to hate him. Nick politely stood and held out an empty chair for her.

"I haven't seen Ray or Janet yet," he said as she sat down. He pushed the menu toward her. "And I haven't ordered. We may as well eat together."

"All right." She could be civilized and adult, too. She took the menu and opened it.

"About last night . . ." he began.

Sarah was glad the menu provided a cover. "You don't—"

"I don't what?"

She lowered the menu. "You don't have to apologize."

Nick's coffee cup clattered into its saucer. "*Apologize?*"

The couple at the next table glanced at them, and then turned away as the waitress approached with a pot of coffee. Sarah handed her the cup and watched as she filled it.

"You changed your mind," she answered. "I don't blame you. We don't know each other that well, and—"

"I didn't change my mind. *You* did."

"I didn't. The door—" She stopped when she saw the incredulous expression cross his face.

"What about the door?"

"It was stuck."

"*Stuck?*"

She nodded. "I called you to see if you could open it from your side, but there was no answer."

The corners of his mouth twitched. "I was taking a cold shower."

Sarah wanted to laugh with relief. "I guess we missed connections."

"I guess we did."

"Maybe it's for the best."

He shook his head, his dark eyes twinkling. "There's still tonight."

They smiled at each other, until Sarah said, "I lied. I didn't sleep well at all."

"Neither did I."

She pretended not to see the gleam in his eyes. Today she would have to get a grip on herself. Making love to Nick couldn't possibly lead to anything but heartache. She would just have to keep reminding herself of that fact.

She tried to change the subject. "I'm looking forward to getting on skis again. I don't remember the last time I went skiing," she said. The waitress took their orders, and hurried away. Sarah glanced around the dining room. "I wonder where Ray and Janet are. It's not like them to be late."

"We should have breakfast and head for the slopes."

"Without them? That wouldn't be right."

"I think it's the best thing to do."

"I should check and see that Janet's all right."

He took a drink of his coffee. "I talked to Ray. I think they've decided to sleep late and ski this afternoon."

Something in his voice made her stare at him. "What is it?"

"Nothing."

"Baloney. You're lousy at keeping secrets."

He fiddled with his fork, obviously stalling. "You saw the way they looked at each other last night."

"Yes. So?"

"Well, *their* door wasn't stuck."

Sarah suddenly realized what he was trying to say. "Ray and Aunt Janet spent the night together?"

"Yes."

"Well," she managed to say, trying to hide her surprise. Of course, they were two adults and could do anything they liked, but Sarah wished she didn't know about it.

"I thought you'd be upset."

"Uh, no. Not anymore. They obviously care for each other very much. It's a little hard to believe they, um, well . . . never mind. Any idea where we're skiing today?"

Nick looked relieved to change the subject. "We'll start slow and work our way down. I picked up a couple of maps of the runs. We'll stay together."

Sarah wasn't sure she agreed with that suggestion. Maybe it would be better to split up for the day. On the other hand, the little adventurous voice inside warned her not to let him out of her sight. "All right," she agreed, taking the plunge. She vowed not to think of the past or worry about the future. "That sounds fine with me."

AND IT WAS, Sarah realized, as they trudged to their rooms that evening. They'd laughed throughout their day together. It had been a day filled with powdery snow and clean mountain air, a day to remember even though now, in the corridor, she realized how tired, cold and hungry she was. Sarah unlocked the door to her room and saw that the connecting door was open, although Nick's door was shut.

"I'm taking no chances," Nick murmured as he followed her into her room. She could tell he meant it and felt unaccustomed heat spread through her. "Just in case."

"How did you fix it?"

Nick unzipped his ski parka and shrugged it off. "I didn't. Maintenance did."

"Ray arranges for songs and you have doors dismantled. I'm impressed." She noticed the message light on the phone was blinking and went over and called the front desk.

"It's our Italian blood. We will do anything to please our women."

She put her hand over the receiver as she waited for the young man on the other end of the line to find her message. "Anything to *seduce* your women, you mean."

"Same thing," he shrugged. "Pleasure, seduction." He smiled as he turned to her. "Would you like me to prove it?"

Sarah wished she could say yes. Instead, she listened to her message and hung up the phone, ignoring his offer. "We'll be late for dinner. The message was from Janet. They're hoping we can meet them at seven."

He looked at his watch and then at Sarah. "That's in half an hour. I'll knock on your door at seven and we'll go down together."

"I'll meet you in the dining room. I'll need plenty of time to soak in the tub and warm up."

He grinned and returned to the hallway door. "I'll be thinking of you the whole time."

"Why aren't you going that way?" She gestured toward the connecting door.

"There's only one reason I'm going to open that door," he said as he left the room. "And that's when you want me as much as I want you."

Oh, she wanted him all right. But that didn't mean she was going to open that door. Sarah hurried into the bathroom. A hot bath would do a lot to ease her tired muscles, but she doubted if she could relax. She didn't even know how she was going to get through dinner.

She turned on the faucets and checked the temperature of the water before stripping off her ski clothes. She was going to live in the present, she reminded herself. And not worry about dinner or later on tonight or anything else in the future. She was in love with the man on the other side of the door, and he seemed pretty crazy about her, too. She was in Colorado, with a private room overlooking the ski slopes, and the only thing she would worry about would be getting to the dining room on time.

She would not worry about making love with Nicholas Ciminero. Whatever happened, happened. For now she intended to be a creature of impulse, a live-for-the-moment free spirit—at least until tomorrow.

IT COULD BE the longest dinner of his life, Nick decided. He attempted to hurry the others through coffee and dessert, but Ray and Janet would not cooperate. In a haze of contentment, they were happy to question Sarah about the day's skiing and the snow conditions and anything else they could think of. They were in no hurry, while Nick wanted only to take Sarah's hand and lead her out of the dining room and straight upstairs to bed.

He'd take his time once he got her alone.

"Well," he tried, during a break in the conversation. "I've had a long day, so I'm going to get to bed early."

Ray didn't pay any attention to him, deciding at that moment to put his arm around Janet and smile at her.

Sarah cleared her throat. "What time shall we meet tomorrow?"

Nick nudged her with his knee. He didn't want to have to get up early in the morning. He had other plans, plans which included waking up beside Sarah.

"Any time, dear," Janet said. "I don't plan on skiing, but I think Ray wants to try."

"We'll see," Ray said. "You two make your own plans. Don't worry about us." It was clear he only wanted to be wherever Janet was.

"That's fine with us," Nick agreed. He stood up and reached for the check. "This one's on me," he said over Ray's protests.

"I'll walk back with you," Sarah offered, and pushed her chair back from the table as she stood up. He liked looking at her, liked the slim brown skirt that grazed the top of her cowboy boots and the matching top with its leather belt. He couldn't decide what article of clothing he'd remove first.

"Good night, dear," Janet said. "You're not going to stay and do a little dancing?"

"We might." Sarah couldn't hide her smile. "But I bet you won't miss us a bit."

Ray winked as he gave Janet's shoulder a squeeze. "You might be right, Sarah."

"Good night, you two."

Nick pulled several bills from his wallet and left them on the table. Then he took Sarah's elbow and led her through the maze of tables, and strode out to the hall. The sound of a slow country waltz came out of the bar, and Nick took Sarah's hand.

"Come on," he urged, tugging her into the dim room to join the other couples on the dance floor. He tucked her into his arms and hummed the words to "Tequila Sunrise" in her ear.

"You have a nice voice," she said, surprised.

He shook his head. "Only in the shower."

"And you like country and western music? I didn't know anyone in Rhode Island listened to that kind of music."

"It's a taste I've acquired here." His hand tightened around her waist. "Among others."

It was heaven in his arms. She loved dancing with him, which is what had tempted her to kick her door down last night. She could have resorted to destruction of property, and all because she'd danced with him.

All because she'd fallen in love with him.

"What are you thinking?" he asked, his voice a warm rumble against the top of her head.

"How did you know I was thinking anything at all?"

"You're always thinking. And worrying."

"How do you know that?"

"I've lived with you for several weeks now. I can tell."

"I was thinking about last night, and how much I wished I could get the door open to see if you had changed your mind."

"About making love to you? I would never change my mind about that." His lips found her forehead and planted a kiss there, then lower, to tickle her earlobe as the singer finished the final verse. Then the band launched into a rowdy two-step, and Nick led Sarah through the crowd toward the door.

"Did you want a drink?"

"No," she answered.

"Neither do I." He kept her hand clasped with his, as if he was afraid she'd change her mind, until they reached the door to her room. She pulled the key from her purse and handed it to him so he could unlock her door. "Shall we try this again? I'll meet you at the other side of the door in fifteen minutes?"

She nodded and pushed the door open. "Make it ten."

"Five."

Sarah shut the door and took a deep breath as she heard him open and close his door. She didn't bother turning on a light. The glow from the outdoor lights alleviated the darkness. She sat on the bed and bent over to tug off her boots.

"One," Nick whispered, as he swung the door open and smiled at her.

"No fair," she said, her hair swinging across her cheek as she struggled with the boot. "It's going to take five minutes for me to get these off."

"I'll help. I've been fantasizing about these boots all through dinner."

"You have?" His openness always surprised her.

"Yeah." He knelt down and grasped her right boot while Sarah leaned back and braced herself as he tugged. "I've always wanted to make love to a cow-girl."

"I'm not exactly a cowgirl."

"Close enough." He set the boots out of the way and stood up. He reached for her and tugged her to her feet, and she went into his arms as his mouth descended on hers. For some irrational reason she felt safe as he held her. He wouldn't hurt her, she knew. And his lips tasted hers with a searing heat that sped throughout the rest of her body with startling swiftness.

He unbuckled her belt and dropped it to the floor. She slid her hands underneath his scratchy wool pull-over to the cotton shirt. All of a sudden it seemed urgent not to wait any longer. She needed to touch him before she lost her courage, before she changed her mind or he changed his. Before they trapped them-selves on either side of a locked door once again.

His fingers grazed the bare skin of her back as he urged the tunic higher, exposing her lace-covered breasts. Sarah worked on releasing the buttons on his shirt until he urged the tunic over her head and tossed that to the floor also. He slid her skirt over her hips. She unbuckled his belt. He kicked off his shoes and she pushed his shirt off his shoulders.

The passion between them, ignited so easily, shouldn't have surprised her. She told herself she should be used to it by now, but still she didn't know how her knees supported her weight. Not when his lips claimed hers again and his large hands grasped her waist, hold-ing her against him as if he would never let her go.

He lifted his head. "No second thoughts?"

She looked up into those dark eyes. She knew there would never be another night in Colorado with Nicholas Ciminero. "No second thoughts," she echoed. He couldn't know that she'd fallen in love with him, wouldn't understand her refusal to admit it.

No second thoughts and no regrets. Just the searing touch of his fingers on her bare skin, and the answering heat from her nearly naked body. *Inevitable*, she realized with a blinding certainty, that they should come together after all. He had known it immediately, and she had refused to see it, denied feeling it.

Until now, as his hands held her and his lips claimed hers and their bodies finally touched in the most intimate of ways. He was hard and warm and solid, and Sarah trembled within his strong embrace. He unhooked her bra, releasing her breasts to the palms of his hands, caressing the softness with a reverent touch as the scrap of lace joined the rest of the clothing on the carpet.

"Beautiful," he murmured. "I knew you would be."

She shook her head. "Don't—"

He smiled, hooking his thumbs underneath the narrow elastic of her underwear and tugging it over her hips. "Don't tell you I think you're beautiful? Impossible."

The darkness helped, eliminating what shyness was left, as Sarah kicked the last piece of her clothing aside. "Your turn," she managed, her voice shaky.

"In a minute," he said, tipping her chin with one long finger. He looked into her eyes. "There's still so many things I don't know about you. Maybe some day you'll trust me enough."

"There isn't anything else you need to know."

He didn't argue, but instead his mouth took hers in a hard, insistent kiss. Somehow they found their way to the bed, and without bothering to turn down the bedspread, tumbled together across the wide expanse of mattress. His lips sought her breasts, sending sweet currents of warmth through her sensitized skin. He stopped to pull off his jeans, then returned to the bed and pulled her to him.

Sarah went willingly into his arms, remembering other times, years ago, when her body seemed to melt underneath her lover's hands. But not like this, when the world tipped crazily out of control and she could hardly breathe for wanting him so badly. But this was different; she was a grown woman, not a carefree teenager with no thought of responsibility for the possible outcome of lovemaking. This time, tonight, there would be no consequences. No risks, except the one to her heart.

And she wouldn't think about that now, not when Nick's strong body pressed heatedly against hers, not when his lips left a trail of fire along her neck and his hands molded her to him. She opened her legs eagerly, welcoming his hard heat between her thighs as her heels touched the calves of his legs and urged him closer.

He parted her, entering in a sure stroke that made her gasp and reach for his shoulders. He moved slowly, carving deeper and deeper until he'd fit himself inside her wet and waiting warmth. Currents of pleasure shot through her, and she instinctively moved to draw him closer.

"I thought you'd feel like this," he murmured into her hair. "Silky. Tight." He moved again, slowly, as if he needed to make sure she was real.

"Nick."

He braced himself on his elbows and looked down at her with dark, hot eyes. "What, love?"

She smiled, and moved her fingers along his smooth cheek. He must have shaved before dinner. "I'm glad you had the door fixed."

His eyes crinkled at the corners and he took her mouth in an endless, drugging kiss as he moved inside her. She arched to meet him, joining him in the timeless rhythm of love, urging him deeper until, long moments later, she tightened around him and thought she would burst with the shocks of pleasure that rippled through her body. He joined her, with a hoarse sound of fulfillment, holding her tightly against him until their breathing slowed.

He nuzzled her neck with tiny kisses while Sarah luxuriated in the feel of his skin underneath her palms. There were no words, but words weren't necessary after all. He stayed inside her, as if unwilling to break the connection between them, as he pulled her onto her side to face him.

He caressed her back with one large hand, skimming along the curve of her spine to the soft swell of her buttocks. "You have such soft skin," he said, wonder in his voice. "And such a beautiful body."

She wriggled slightly as his hand cupped her and held her against him. She felt him harden and swell inside her. "So do you," she murmured, touching his face. He moved within her, strong and sure.

"This time," he promised, "we're going to go slow. I want to discover everything you like."

"I think," Sarah said, gasping slightly at the heavy presence within her, "I think I'm going to like everything we do."

NICK EASED HIMSELF from the rumpled bed and stared at the sleeping woman tangled in the white sheets. Her dark hair skimmed the pillow and brushed her naked shoulders, making him long to wake her and start all over again.

But he wouldn't wake her, even if he thought he could find the strength to make love with her once more. It had been a night of discovery, with hours spent exploring, touching, tasting and moving together, skin against skin. Now, as he pulled the drapes back, dawn lit the sky with the promise of a new day.

A new day. He should be glad to see it, but after breakfast they would pack to leave, head east to North Platte and then, who knew? He dropped the curtain back in place and looked back at the sleeping woman. His options were limited. Talking her into staying here for a few more days was out of the question; he knew she'd never agree to taking time off from school, especially now. Even if he wanted to head back to Rhode Island, he was out of a job until the beginning of the new year.

And he didn't know how he could leave her.

He'd thought the last thing he'd expected to happen in Nebraska was to fall in love, but he was wrong. Nick sighed and ran his fingers through his rumpled hair. The last thing he'd expected was to enjoy it.

He stepped closer to the bed and decided to join Sarah for a few more hours' sleep. One thing he knew for certain, he realized as he slid closer to the warm heat of her nude body, he was never going to let her go.

SARAH AWOKE with Nick's arms wrapped around her, her body snuggled against his under the warm cocoon of sheets and blankets. She thought she'd be embarrassed, but instead she felt content and peaceful.

And sad, too, she decided, closing her eyes against the morning light. There wouldn't be another morning in Nick's arms, no more nights spent making love with this special man who'd arrived in her life so unexpectedly. He had a life elsewhere, and she had her life and her work in Nebraska.

There had never been any talk of the future; she didn't expect it. This had been a weekend to live in the present. There was no way of knowing what the future held unless the Ghost of Christmas Future appeared in person to give her a quick prediction.

"I HAVE AN ANNOUNCEMENT to make," Ray said suddenly, setting his coffee cup down with a clatter on the kitchen table. "I've decided I'm not going back."

"Not going back where?" Nick asked. He knew his hours without sleep were catching up with him; it felt like midnight instead of six o'clock, but he must have missed part of the conversation. Was it possible to fall asleep while eating a roast beef sandwich?

"I'm not going back to Providence."

"What?" Nick looked from Ray's determined expression to Janet's incredulous one. Obviously she hadn't known Ray's plans either.

"I'm retiring. I've given it a lot of thought these past weeks, so don't try to talk me out of it."

"You're not the type of man to retire," Nick protested. "You always said you couldn't hang around Miami Beach with nothing to do."

"I'm not going to hang around Miami Beach. First thing tomorrow morning I'm calling a real estate agent and start looking for a house right here."

Nick stared at him, wondering if the old man had finally turned the corner into fantasyland. "*Here?*"

"In North Platte?" Sarah asked. "Are you sure you want to live in such a cold place?"

Ray reached across the table and took Janet's hand. "I want to live wherever Janet lives. I've had more fun these past weeks than I've had in many, many years."

Janet blushed, but she didn't take her hand away from his.

"But what about the business?"

"Ah," Ray said, turning an assessing gaze toward Nick. "I knew we'd come to that. I'm selling out." He held up one hand as if to ward off Nick's protest. "You and I will talk about it in private, but you're welcome to buy me out, if that's what you want to do."

"*If* that's what I want?" Nick frowned. "Are you feeling all right?"

"Never better, son." Ray grinned. "Never better."

Nick's head began to pound. "I wish we could all say the same," he muttered. He couldn't wait to talk to Ray and find out what all this was about.

AN HOUR LATER, in the privacy of Ray's bedroom, he found out.

"There's no mystery," Ray stated, still looking pleased with himself. "I've looked into the future without Janet and decided I didn't like what I saw."

"Which was?"

"Living alone. Dying alone." His dark eyes grew serious. "I've wasted too many years chasing the dollar, son. There aren't that many years left, so I'm going to do what I want."

"Which is to sell Sandetti Specialties?"

He nodded. "Among other things. It's yours, if you want it."

"I want it," Nick said through gritted teeth. "But—"

"No." He turned away and reached for the doorknob. "There's nothing you can say that will change my mind, Niccolo." He turned back to Nick before he opened the door. "But if I were you I'd think long and hard on if I'd want to marry a business. You know what's involved, and you know how many hours you work to make it a success. I've given my life to it. Don't give it yours."

"You gave your life to it because you loved it."

Ray shrugged. "Possibly. Or perhaps it kept me so busy I didn't have time to realize that my heart was empty." He pointed to Nick's chest. "You listen to your heart, Niccolo. If you have to choose between your woman and your business, think very hard before you choose what can't keep you warm at night."

"I can have both."

"Perhaps you can. You've never had a family, though. And neither have I. If you want Sandetti Specialties you're welcome to it. If you can afford it."

"I want it," Nick growled. "At any price."

Ray shook his head. "The money is not what I'm talking about. You are like a son to me, so of course I'll make it easy for you. But there will be other prices to pay. For your sake I hope they won't be too high."

SARAH LINGERED over the dishes, wiping the counters several times before she realized she was simply stalling, hoping Nick would return and tell her what was going on. Janet wasn't saying much; she'd simply smiled and said she was going to bed early.

Nick's expression had been stunned when Ray announced his intention to sell the business and move to North Platte permanently. Clearly the brief interlude in Nebraska was nothing more than that. If in some tiny part of her heart she'd hoped he'd stay, she now knew that had been a silly fantasy. The man loved his work, loved his life back East and all it entailed. When Ray announced he was going to sell, Nick looked as if Ray had cut his heart out and set it on the kitchen table.

She squeezed the excess water from the sponge and set it by the faucet, then released the water in the sink and watched it disappear with a gurgling sound. The rest of the house was quiet. Too quiet, the way it had been before the two men had landed on the doorstep.

Which was beginning to feel like a hundred years ago. She didn't want to imagine what it would be like when they left. But then again, Ray wasn't going very far. He'd most likely be a frequent guest, an honorary uncle who'd come to the football parties and the holiday dinners. And if he and Aunt Janet chose to sleep together, that was their business. Sarah vowed to mind her own business, especially in that area.

"Sarah?"

She turned around as Nick entered the kitchen. He looked tired, distracted, until he smiled at her. "It's been one hell of a day. I wish we were back in Denver."

"Me, too," she answered softly.

"I don't suppose I could convince you to sleep on the third floor tonight?"

She shook her head. "No. Last night was something I'll always remember, but it can't continue."

"No?" His expression darkened. "I thought it was just the beginning."

"I never said that."

"You didn't have to. One-night stands are not my style."

"Or mine."

"Then what are you saying?"

"It was just..." She struggled for words. "Just something special, something that can't happen again. We're too different, and we live in two different worlds." She dried her hands on the dish towel and watched him walk closer to her.

"I'm buying the business," he stated, putting his hands on her shoulders.

"Yes, I thought you would."

"Come back to Rhode Island with me."

"What?" What was he talking about?

"Come back with me. Move there."

"You know I can't."

"All right. We can wait until the end of the school year, if we have to."

"I can't move to Rhode Island, Nick." She stared up at him, as surprised by his suggestion as she had been by Ray's announcement of his retirement. "What are you talking about?"

"Marriage," he replied, his dark eyes shining down at her. "Marry me, Sarah. I'll buy you a house by the ocean. In fact, I've even seen a house that would be a perfect place to raise a family. Until now, until I met you, I didn't know that something important was missing from my life. All this time I've concentrated on making money and everything else I thought was important. Now I know differently."

"Nick, we don't know each other."

One eyebrow lifted. "After last night you can say that? I know your scent, how you taste and how you feel. I know how you move underneath me and above me and around me." His eyes darkened. "You don't know everything about me, true. I'm an orphan, raised in a boys' home, tossed out on my own when I was eighteen. Does that make me a lousy prospective husband?"

"No. Of course not."

"You know I've made myself what I am—I didn't have any other choice. But all that I have now is yours, Sarah, if you'll come with me. I think I fell in love with you the moment I saw you, but I was too stupid to see it."

"Love isn't the answer, Nick. This is just a few days—"

"Weeks," he corrected.

She continued as if she hadn't heard him interrupt. "—of infatuation, of romance. That doesn't mean we have enough to build a life together."

"Why not? What more do you need?"

"I need to stay here, for one thing. Janet took me in when I had no place to go. She put me through college. I can't leave her now. She's had her share of problems with her health and she needs me. She can't stay in this house alone without me."

"Surely she expected you to marry someday."

"I'm sure she didn't expect me to move halfway across the country, even if I wanted to. Which I don't." She touched her finger to his lips. "Don't say anything until I've finished, please?" She took her finger away and felt her heart shatter and break as she looked into his eyes. He was hurt and angry and frustrated, and there was nothing she could do about it except refuse to drag out the pain. "We're too different. And our lives are too far apart. I can't leave what I have here and you can't leave the business you've worked so hard to build.

You're an ambitious, successful, brilliant man—that's the kind of life you need."

"Live it with me."

"No," she whispered. "I can't."

"Do you think I'm going to take no for an answer?"

"It would be easier if you would. I should have known you wouldn't understand."

"What is *that* supposed to mean?"

She was treading on dangerous ground, and she fought to keep control of her emotions. She lowered her voice. "If you've never had a family, it's hard to explain what it means. It's a matter of loyalty."

"That's a low blow, Sarah."

"It's the truth."

He shook his head, as if he couldn't believe she would refuse the chance for a life with him. "There has to be more to this than you're telling me."

"Don't make this so hard, Nick," she begged.

He planted a brief kiss on her lips before releasing her. "I intend to make it a lot harder, Sarah. When I leave here, you'll be with me."

Sarah watched him stride out of the kitchen before she swallowed the lump in her throat. She would never leave Nebraska, and she couldn't tell him why.

11

"I CAN'T make up my mind," Ray grumbled, sorting through the stack of papers on the couch. "I've looked at seven houses this week and there's something wrong with each one."

"I'm going back to Rhode Island," Nick said, deliberately ignoring Ray's discussion of real estate.

"No, you're not. You're going to stick around and help me find a house."

"I don't work for you anymore, remember?"

"Fine," Ray grumbled. "I'm hiring you back. Your first job is to help me find a house. Everything's too big or too far away."

"Too far away from what?"

"From this house. I want something close by."

"How close?"

"Next door would be ideal, but the houses around here are just too big. I don't want anything I'm going to rattle around in."

"I think you've lost your mind, Ray. You can move to North Platte, but you don't have to sell the business. Retire, if you want, but don't sell something you've spent your life on." Nick shoved his hands in the pockets of his jeans and stared out the window at the snow falling on the front lawn. "This is crazy. I don't know what I'm doing here anymore."

"Yes, you do. There's a pretty little schoolteacher who's on her way home now, that's what. Why don't you just marry her and get on with it?"

"I've asked her to marry me. She said no."

Ray looked surprised. "Why? I thought you two were getting along just fine."

"She won't leave Janet. And she thinks she and I are too different."

"Bull."

"Yeah," Nick agreed. "But she's been avoiding me all week. I can't even get her alone to argue about it." He turned to Ray. "You, on the other hand, don't seem to be having any trouble with your romance."

Ray smiled. "After forty-eight years, son, a man should know how to proceed. Besides, you've been talking to the lawyers so I haven't had much to do except watch Janet bake Christmas cookies." He smiled to himself. "It's been a good week."

"I should fly back and see how everything is going."

"You spend four or five hours a day on that phone. And they've faxed you the important things. What good would it do to leave now, especially if you're trying to convince Sarah to marry you? Out of sight, out of mind, son. I'm warning you, and I should know."

"What happened during the war, Ray? You've never said much except that you were a medic assigned to the marines in the South Pacific."

"The war isn't important, Niccolo. And next year isn't either. It's today that matters, because there aren't any guarantees about tomorrow."

"The Ghost of Christmas Present," Nick mused.

"What?"

Nick shook his head. "Never mind. I was thinking of *A Christmas Carol*. I just seem to be hearing a lot about that particular ghost lately."

THE WEEK CRAWLED BY. Ray bounced in and out of the house, discussing homes with Janet and sampling the different kinds of cookies she continued to turn out. Rehearsals continued for the Christmas pageant, despite an outbreak of stomach flu and the excitement of the impending holiday. The children were practically bouncing off the walls; Sarah had her hands full trying to keep order. Still, she envied them their excitement, with Christmas vacation so close. She wished she didn't dislike this time of year so much, but she couldn't help remembering the final month of her pregnancy. She'd known she would be giving up her baby and life would never be the same again.

"Sarah?"

She looked up from her paperwork as Janet, in her pink bathrobe and slippers, pushed open the bedroom door and stepped inside the room.

"Do you mind if we talk for a moment?"

"Of course not." Sarah looked at the clock. After eleven already. No wonder she'd been yawning. "I didn't know it was so late. What are you doing up?"

"Ray and I were talking in the living room. I saw your light and thought I'd say good-night." She patted Sarah's back. "Are you all right, dear?"

"Sure, everything's fine." *I've fallen in love with the wrong man. Again. But everything's fine.*

"Really?"

"Really," Sarah assured her. There wasn't anything she could do except act normal. Like nothing had ever happened. Still, it was practically impossible to forget the hours in Nick's arms, their time together in Colorado, or the moment when he asked her to marry him. And the expression on his face when she'd refused.

Janet sat down on the bed. "You've been so quiet this week. And you haven't been home much. Have you and Nick quarreled?"

"Not really. You know how busy this time of year is. And the show is taking up a lot of time after school."

"Next Saturday it will be over and you can enjoy the holidays. We're looking forward to it."

"I'll make sure you and Ray get front-row seats."

"What do you think about Ray's staying in town? I know it was a surprise to you, but I was so happy he decided to stay. He really is a dear friend."

Sarah couldn't help but tease her. "A friend, Aunt Janet? Are you sure that's all it is, friendship?"

Janet shook her head. "I didn't come in here to talk about me or Ray. It's you I'm concerned about. Nick is such a fine young man, and the two of you seem to get along so well. Is there anything you need to talk about?"

"No. Nothing at all." Sarah softened the answer with a smile and stood up to give her aunt a kiss on the cheek. "Now, go get some rest. You've been doing too much baking."

"There's no such thing, not at Christmastime. Cookies seem to disappear as fast as I bake them."

"Because you give them away."

"I've frozen quite a few," she protested before she realized Sarah was teasing.

"Go to bed," Sarah ordered. "And I will, too."

"That's a good idea," she agreed, sliding off the bed. "This time of year is entirely too much fun."

"Good night."

"Good night, dear. See you in the morning."

"Probably not. I'll be heading out early again."

Janet shot her a concerned look. "He won't wait around forever, you know."

"I know." But he'd said he'd stay around long enough to make sure he couldn't get his own way. Part of her wished he'd leave, although she knew she would miss him forever.

She knew he hadn't believed her refusal to marry him. Anger, disappointment, then resolve had been easy to recognize now that she knew him so well. He wouldn't give up; she was sure of that. He was the kind of man who always got what he wanted. But this time it wasn't going to happen.

She'd fallen in love with him, but she wasn't ready to give up her life here, and she couldn't leave Aunt Janet. Nick didn't understand that, because he'd never had a family, but Sarah knew all too well what having a family meant. Her mother had died, her father had turned his back on her, and Janet was the only person who had welcomed a pregnant teenager with open arms. She didn't blame her father anymore, but she wished things had been different. She couldn't imagine taking Janet and moving to Rhode Island either, especially not with Ray moving here. Janet's family was here, her life was here. *But is mine?*

She couldn't tell Nick about her baby, either. How would he ever understand? The picture tucked inside the desk drawer stayed in its place. It was too painful to look at the tiny sleeping face of her day-old daughter. The child she'd given birth to would celebrate her birthday soon. Sarah tried not to give in to her grief. She'd made a life for herself: gone to college, had a job she loved. But still, eleven years was a long time to be alone.

"ARE YOU GOING IN or coming out?"

"Out." Sarah backed out of the closet, pulling a carton of Christmas ornaments with her. *Darn*. She'd done a great job of avoiding him up until now.

Nick's voice came closer. "Need help?"

"No. There's no sense in both of us getting dirty," she answered, reaching for her flashlight. She swung it around the dark corners of the storage area, hoping she hadn't missed any of the boxes of Christmas decorations. Janet always insisted on decorating the house, leaving no room untouched by Christmas spirit. Satisfied, Sarah finished climbing out of the eaves and shut the small door.

"Looks like you're getting ready for the holidays," Nick stated as he reached down to give her a hand. She grasped it and hauled herself to her feet.

"Janet likes to decorate."

"I'll carry them down for you."

"No, that's okay. They're not heavy." She avoided his gaze, bending down to pick up a carton instead.

"Sarah," he said, stopping her by taking the box from her arms and putting it back on the floor. "I'm going back to Rhode Island today."

Sarah stared at him. She should have been relieved at the announcement, but her heart dropped to her toes. "So this is goodbye," she managed.

He gripped her shoulders so she couldn't walk away. "You've been avoiding me. What else do you want me to do?"

"Nothing. It's better this way."

Nick shook his head. "That's where you're wrong, Sarah. I love you. That's not going to change right away. But I have a lot of work to do now that I'm buying the business, and Ray and I both want it settled as soon as possible."

"I see."

"No, I doubt that you do. I'm coming back," he promised. "I wouldn't miss *A Christmas Carol*." He kissed her, a hard kiss that promised everything, but was over long before Sarah wanted it to end.

"Are you staying for Christmas?"

"I don't know. I guess that depends on whether you'll marry me."

"Nick, you know I can't—"

"I'll be back," he repeated, his face unsmiling. "By then both of us should know what we're doing."

Sarah watched as he picked up his suitcase and went down the stairs. She looked around the attic bedroom, Nick's home for the past several weeks. It was spotless, completely devoid of any reminder of Nicholas Ciminero. He'd said he would return, but Sarah didn't know whether or not she wanted to believe him. Neither alternative would be easy.

"WHAT HAPPENED to all of the letters I wrote, Janet? Did you throw them away?"

"No, of course not." She put the rolling pin down, willingly interrupting the morning's work. She'd been waiting for this question for weeks. The only surprise was that it had taken so long for him to ask. "I have them all." She untied her apron, went upstairs to her bedroom and retrieved the box of letters from the shelf in her closet. When she returned to the kitchen, she sat beside Ray at the table and placed the box in front of him.

"I kept yours, too," he said, touching the box. "What was left of them, that is. The jungle claimed too many."

"Go ahead, open it. They're your letters, after all."

Ray lifted the lid with shaking hands, then stopped when he saw the packets tied with faded pink ribbons. "I don't know if I can."

"Here," she said, "I'll help." Janet brushed at her eyes and reached for them, setting the packets on the table and putting the empty box on the floor. "I kept them in order." She handed him a thick bundle. "This is 1943."

He untied the ribbon, picked up the first V-mail letter and unfolded it. He read silently for a minute, then looked over at Janet. "I was very young, wasn't I?"

She smiled, remembering. "To a sixteen-year-old you were a very mature older man."

"I grew up fast over there."

"Yes. By the time the war was over, you were a man with plans and dreams."

"A man who loved you." He shook his head and reached for another packet. "I shouldn't have pressured you," he muttered. "I realize that now."

"We both know a lot of things we didn't know then," she answered.

For long moments he looked through the piles of letters, until he came to a small packet held together with a rubber band. "These aren't opened. Why not?" He didn't wait for an answer, but examined the postmarks. "These are the ones I wrote from Rhode Island. You never opened them?"

She put her hand on his. "I never got them."

"How can that be? They're right here. I even sent you train tickets—" He searched through the letters until he found the one he wanted. He opened the envelope and pulled the tickets out. "See? I told you to bring your sisters and come to me."

"I didn't know." Janet couldn't control the tears that ran down her cheeks, and reached for Ray. "Don't you see? I didn't know." He put his arms around her and held her against him, not caring that his tears mingled with hers.

Ray let her cry, and when her tears finally stopped he patted her back and then pulled away so he could look down at her face. "I think you'd better tell me what happened."

"LOUDER," Sarah whispered, hoping Tiny Tim would hear her and raise her voice. Not one fifth-grade boy had consented to play a character called Tiny Tim, so little Brenda Svoboda took the part. Unfortunately, her voice was as little as the rest of her, but she valiantly spouted her lines as best she could. When she had finished, the Cratchit family did a dance to a Rolling Stones song, "You Can't Always Get What You Want."

The audience's chuckles turned into laughter as they recognized the music. Sarah waved to Tony, and he pushed the button on his boom-box and stopped the recording. The curtain closed, and applause followed the end of the opening act.

Sarah stood by the curtains, out of sight of the audience of enthusiastic parents, ready to cue lines and scene endings. So far, so good. Betty had volunteered to help with the costume changes, and one of the mothers stood backstage to keep the children quiet. Now the Ghost of Christmas Past would make his appearance, forcing Scrooge to confront his mistakes. Sarah peered through the curtain to see if Ray and Janet were enjoying the show as special guests with front-row seats, and she caught a glimpse of Nick bending over to talk to them as he took his seat beside them.

She'd felt foolish saving a seat for someone who was sixteen hundred miles away, but Janet had insisted. Now she realized Janet had more faith in Nick's promise than she did.

"What are you smiling about?" Betty asked.

"Nick came back to see the show."

"He didn't come back to North Platte to see the show. He came for *you*. When are you going to put the man out of his misery and marry him?"

"I should never have told you about that."

"You need me," Betty grinned. "I'm the one who believes in romance and love at first sight and all that good stuff. Changed your mind?"

"Not right now," Sarah said. "I have a show to do." She watched to see that the children were in place and Scrooge was in his bed before she gave the signal to open the curtains.

The rest of the performance went well, despite a minor altercation between Scrooge and a "mourner" with a tombstone. Even the Ghost of Christmas Future remembered her lines. Tony had arranged the music with a bouncy combination of hard rock and rap. Scrooge realized his mistakes and set out to make up for his behavior until the grand finale when the chorus, led by a jubilant Mr. Scrooge and a very nervous Tiny Tim, sang "Deck The Halls." Tiny Tim urged the audience to join in, which led to Betty's class taking over the songfest. Sarah breathed a sigh of relief, resolving to stick to making holiday wreaths next year and stay out of show business. Soon, the curtains closed and the lights went on and Betty invited the families in the audience to the cafeteria for punch and cookies.

Sarah stalled as long as she could, but it didn't take long for the actors and actresses to hurry out of their costumes and join their parents for holiday treats. Sarah intended to make her way through the crowd to join Ray and Janet, but Nick met her outside the cafeteria.

"Nice job," he said. "The play was, uh, everything I thought it would be." His eyes danced. "Especially when the Ghost of Christmas Future did that rap dance. I thought it was a nice touch."

Sarah chuckled. "She insisted on it, so Tony came up with the music."

"Well," he said, taking her arm. "It was very creative."

"And full of Christmas spirit," she added. "At least, I hope the parents thought so."

"The parents thought it was great. Listen, Sarah—"

"Miss McGrath! Miss McGrath! My grandma wants to meet you!" Brenda called, running up to Sarah.

"All right," Sarah agreed. She looked back at Nick. "I'll see you back at the house."

He nodded. "Want me to give you a ride home?"

"No, I'm all set." Brenda tugged an older woman toward Sarah, and Sarah had no time to wonder why Nick had returned.

By THE TIME she finally returned home, the lights in all the windows were lit, including the electric candles Janet liked to place in each window. Christmas music greeted her when she opened the front door and stepped inside. The entry looked festive, with garlands of greenery and fat red bows draped over the staircase banister. With only eight days left until Christmas, Janet had thrown herself into decorating for the holiday, with Ray her willing assistant. Yesterday the two of them had managed to drag a tree into the corner of the living room, but Janet had refused to decorate it until Nick returned. She and Ray had made popcorn balls instead.

Janet came out of the kitchen carrying a tray loaded with cookies and four coffee cups. "Hi, dear! We've been waiting for you!"

"Let me take that," Sarah ordered. "And waiting for me? Why?"

"We're ready to decorate the tree and we couldn't start without you."

"Oh." She followed Janet into the living room. Ray and Nick faced each other on opposite sofas, and they looked pleased. Sarah assumed that their business plans were going well. Janet set the tray on the low table between the sofas. "Okay, you two. Quit talking business and help yourselves to coffee and cookies."

"Then we'll decorate the tree?" Nick asked.

"You can start any time you want," Janet assured him. "Ray and I hung the lights and the garland this afternoon. Those small boxes by the fireplace are the ones with the ornaments."

Nick hesitated, looking very much like a ten-year-old trying not to get into trouble. "You don't mind if I help?"

"Of course not. Why would I?"

Because, Sarah realized, he'd been a little boy without a family. Without family traditions and musty boxes of holiday decorations and a dining room table lined with relatives. Everywhere he went he was a guest, and guests didn't hang other people's Christmas ornaments.

"I'll help, too," Sarah offered, grabbing a star-shaped cookie dusted with red sugar as she passed the coffee table.

Janet sat down beside Ray. "We'll watch you young people for a while," she said, leaning forward for her cup. "The show was wonderful, Sarah. It's always wonderful."

Sarah took a bite of the cookie, then unwrapped a ceramic Santa Claus and hooked it on the tree. "Thanks. This year's class is a great group of kids. I have trouble keeping one step ahead of them."

Ray chuckled. "That Tiny Tim was sure cute."

"Brenda. She's my cousin's child," Janet said. "I recognized quite a few familiar faces in the crowd."

Sarah watched Nick take a rocking horse from its box and hang it carefully on a heavy branch. He turned to see Sarah watching him. "Am I doing this right?"

"Sure." She unwrapped a toy soldier and handed it to him.

"You have a lot of ornaments."

She reached into the box for another one. "Lots of my kids have given me ornaments for Christmas."

"And she uses every single one of them," Janet added. "It's a good thing we have high ceilings and can put up a big tree."

Nick started to relax, pleased he hadn't broken anything. "Want to pass the cookies? This is going to take a while."

Janet stood up and handed him the tray. "Put it there, on the chair, if you want. I'm going to put some Christmas music on the record player."

"You have a record player?"

"I'm too old to start with all that new stuff," she answered. "I like my records just fine."

Nick and Sarah finished decorating the tree in silence, with the music playing softly in the background and Ray and Janet content to watch. It had been worth

the long day of flying, Nick decided, to have an evening like this. He was bone-weary, exhausted from trying to cram four weeks of work into ten days. If he
hadn't promised Sarah he'd come back for her show,
he would have buried himself in work until after New
Year's and never even noticed the holidays. Come to
think of it, some of Scrooge's behavior tonight seemed
embarrassingly familiar.

When the tree was finished, Nick plugged in the
lights, Sarah put the boxes in the hall, Janet turned off
all the living room lamps, and the four of them sat
down to admire the twinkling tree.

"We forgot the popcorn balls," Ray said. He reached
for the basket on the table beside him. "Janet and I made
a special treat. Who wants one?"

"I'll wait, thanks," Sarah said.

Nick grinned. "Toss me one. That sounds good."

"Not good for your teeth," Janet chuckled. "But Ray
insisted."

Ray handed Janet a cellophane-wrapped ball.
"There's yours. I wrapped it myself."

"It's too pretty to eat," she said, holding it in her
hands. "Maybe I'll hang it on the tree instead."

Ray put his arm around her. "What did you say to me
so many years ago? 'Make sure you eat every bite'?" At
Janet's curious look, he urged, "Go ahead."

She untied the ribbon, unwrapped the cellophane
and noticed the ball had been cut in half. She pried the
pieces apart to discover a small velvet box nestled inside.

"Open it," Ray urged.

Janet lifted the hinged lid to reveal a gold ring blaz-
ing with yellow sapphires and diamonds. She slowly

removed it from the box and watched the stones reflect the twinkling lights of the Christmas tree. "Ray! What on earth—"

"I've asked you once before," he said, "and Lord knows you've had enough time to think about it. Will you marry me?"

"Oh, yes," she answered, her eyes bright with unshed tears. "I certainly will."

He slid the ring on her finger and kissed her gently, then whispered in her ear before turning to the younger couple standing mesmerized by the tree. "This calls for a celebration, don't you think?"

"I certainly do," Nick agreed, stepping forward to shake Ray's hand. "Congratulations," he said, leaning over to kiss Janet's cheek. Sarah was right behind him, kissing Janet and hugging Ray.

"Let's celebrate officially." Ray left the room and returned with a tray carrying a bottle of champagne and four glasses. "I feel a little bit like Scrooge tonight."

Sarah laughed. "For heaven's sake, why?"

He brought Janet's hand to his lips and kissed it ever so gently. "Because he was a mean old man who came to his senses and got a second chance."

Ray unwrapped the top of the champagne bottle, popped the cork and began to pour the bubbly liquid into the glasses. Then he stood up. "I'd like to propose a toast to my future bride." He beamed at the younger couple.

"Hear, hear," Nick said. "This is great news. I wish you both much happiness," he said, clinking his glass with Ray's, then Janet's.

Sarah couldn't help smiling. "I think it's wonderful, Aunt Janet and *Uncle* Ray. You two are amazing."

"Yes," Nick agreed, coming to stand beside Sarah and putting his arm around her waist. "Amazing is a good word for the two of them. When's the wedding?"

Janet blushed and smiled at Ray, then turned to Nick and Sarah. "We haven't talked about that yet."

"*I*'ve given it some thought."

Janet chuckled, looking down at the beautiful ring on her finger. "Yes, Ray, I'm sure you have. When are we getting married?"

"We don't want to waste any time. So we're going to be married on Christmas Eve."

Sarah almost choked. "But that's only six days from now!"

Ray nodded. "It's a special anniversary for us. We'll have plenty of time to get our blood tests and apply for the marriage license."

"All right," Janet agreed, her eyes shining. "Christmas Eve it is."

"Well, it's up to you two. It certainly sounds wonderful," Sarah said. "What kind of wedding do you want? When are you going to tell the rest of the family?"

Nick studied Sarah as the discussion turned to wedding plans. Now she could have no reason to refuse to marry him. That was the best Christmas present of all.

12

"Good," Nick said an hour later, satisfaction in his voice as he joined Sarah on the couch. "We're finally all alone."

"I'm surprised you came back. You were pretty angry when you left."

"Not angry as much as frustrated. I missed you too much to stay angry with you." He put his arm around her and drew her close. "I promised you I'd come back for the show, didn't I? And I wanted to do this," he said, kissing her softly on the lips before continuing. "And this." He touched her cheek and tucked one strand of chestnut hair behind her ear with a gentle finger. "I've thought about our night in Colorado, over and over again. I couldn't stop remembering how soft your skin was and how much I wanted to please you."

Sarah sighed and moved closer to him. "You did."

He dragged his lips along her jaw, then nipped at her earlobe, inhaling the faint scent of perfume. "I remembered how you tasted."

"Nick—"

"Are you on vacation?"

"Um, yes. Until January third."

"You can sleep late in the morning?"

"Yes. Tomorrow's Sunday."

"I forgot." He forced himself off the couch and tugged Sarah to her feet. "Come on. You're sleeping in my bed tonight." He didn't get the argument he expected. Not that he was going to listen to how different they were and how they had nothing in common. That didn't matter anymore. He loved her, and he had a pretty good idea that she was in love with him, too.

"Nick," she tried, as they climbed the stairs.

"Shh," he warned. "We don't want to wake Janet."

They tiptoed along the hall, past the door to Sarah's bedroom, up the stairs to the third floor, then reached the wide room with its large bed tucked against the end wall. "There," he said. "This is what I've been fantasizing about. You, me and that bed."

"You have a thing for beds."

"We almost did it in the kitchen a few times," he reminded her as he shut the door behind them.

"I like the bed better," Sarah murmured, going willingly into his arms, telling herself she could stop at any time. But she knew she wouldn't want to. She'd tried so hard to pretend that it didn't matter that he'd left, that she would be fine if he never returned, but it wasn't true. She'd missed him more than she had ever dreamed she could miss someone. For a little while longer, he was still in her life. And she decided she'd better enjoy being with him, at least one more time.

He undressed her then, unbuttoning her red knit dress and sliding it off, kissing each bare shoulder before moving lower, sending shivers along her spine. When she would have reached for him, he shook his head. "No," he whispered. "You don't have to move."

Her bra fluttered to the carpet, and his lips moved over her breasts in startling, heated patterns, urging the peaks to harden against his tongue. Then lower, his fingers stripped off the rest of her clothing to pool at her feet.

She reached for him then, wanting to feel his skin against hers. "My turn," she said, sliding her palms along his shirt.

"Not yet. I've missed the taste of you," he said, stepping backward to sit on the bed. He held her between his knees and feathered kisses against her abdomen, sending flutters along her skin and causing her to grip his shoulders to keep from falling. He made love to her with his lips and his tongue, finding her secret places and invading with an intimate touch that left her breathless. Desire, hot and heavy, coursed through her as they tumbled together on the bed.

She reached for him, unbuckling his belt with urgent fingers until she found the long, satin length of him and released him, hot and hard against her palm.

"Come here," he rasped, pulling her on top of him. She went willingly, guiding him into her while her hair fell against his shoulders. He took her mouth as he took her body, with tantalizing strokes that went on and on. Sarah clung to him, sure she would never know this kind of passion again and reluctant to let it end. Long moments later, whatever control she clung to washed away in a long, shattering climax that rocked them both.

Sarah sighed with contentment and nuzzled kisses along his neck. Making love with Nick had been her very own private Christmas present, and she didn't regret it. She smiled down into his eyes. "At least we made it onto the bed," she said.

"Next time I'll take my clothes off," he promised, tumbling her onto her side. He tucked her hair behind her ear.

"And when exactly is next time, Mr. Ciminero?"

"Keep looking at me like that and you won't sleep at all tonight."

"I hadn't planned to."

He smiled, his hand tracing the gentle dip of her waist. "Neither had I," he said, pulling her closer to him. "Neither had I."

"TAKE IT AWAY," Sarah begged. "I can't eat any more."

Nick chuckled and pushed the package of cookies aside. "But you were having such a good time."

She licked pink frosting from her fingers. "You shouldn't have brought me a whole box."

"I brought you *three* boxes," he admitted. "The other two are still in my suitcase."

"You are a *wonderful* man." She nestled against the pillows, the covers pulled over her breasts. "You know all of my weaknesses, don't you?"

"I'm learning."

"Umm," she sighed, obviously content to stay with him all night. "Like I said, you're wonderful."

"Then you'll marry me?"

Her eyes flew open. "Nick," she began, her voice hesitant. "I told you, I—"

"Janet won't be alone anymore," he said, climbing off the bed and wrapping his bathrobe around him. "You can't use that as an excuse."

"It wasn't an excuse."

"Then say yes." Nick sat next to her on the bed and waited. He didn't like the way she hesitated.

"I can't."

"We love each other."

"Yes." She didn't look at him when she answered.

"But you won't marry me. First you said you couldn't leave your aunt alone. Now she won't be alone. She's going to live happily ever after with Ray. You can visit here, and Ray and Janet will visit us. So what's the reason now?"

"I'm not going to get into this." Sarah started to push the covers away, but Nick was faster, using his weight to pin the blankets around her so she couldn't get out of the bed.

"Not so fast," he muttered. "You're not running away from this, not anymore. You can't make love to me like we just did and then get up and leave. I'm offering you everything I have, everything I am. Unconditional love, Sarah. What's wrong with that?"

"I *do* love you," she admitted in a choked voice. "But—"

"But not enough," he finished for her. "I'm not good enough for you? Is that the reason?" Sarah started to protest, but he rose, releasing her.

"No, Nick," she said softly, leaving the bed. She picked up her clothes and moved toward the door. "It's the other way around."

He didn't watch her leave, but he heard her quiet footsteps descend the staircase and the click of her bedroom door as it closed.

First thing in the morning he would get the next available flight East. He didn't know what secrets Sarah harbored, but now he was certain that something more than loyalty to her aunt held her back from marrying him.

Nick tossed the suitcase on the bed and glared at it. What was wrong with him? He wanted a family. One of his own. He wanted children, hopefully a boy and a girl. He wanted Sarah's face to be the first thing he saw in the morning and the last one at night. He wanted her with him always, but damn—why couldn't he convince her that it would all work out?

Maybe he was better off just going back to Rhode Island and forgetting everything that happened here. After all, he really didn't have any other choice.

If she didn't want him, there was nothing else he could do to convince her. It was the story of his life.

"SARAH!"

Sarah rolled onto her side and pulled the covers over her shoulder. It was almost dawn, and she thought she'd finally drifted off to sleep after tossing and turning for hours. Her aunt's voice must be part of her dream, she decided, until she heard the undercurrent of fear in the word. "Sarah? Sarah!"

She leapt to her feet and hurried across the hall to Janet's room. "Aunt Janet? What's wrong?"

"I'm not sure," she gasped, as if she couldn't get enough air. Sarah rushed to the bed and switched the light on. Janet was pale, with tinges of gray around her mouth.

"Your heart?" She tried to hide the fear that gripped her.

Janet nodded. "I hoped it would go away, but it isn't."

Nick appeared in the doorway, fully dressed, as if he'd been waiting for dawn. "I'll call an ambulance," he said, hurrying to the phone near the bed. "We'll get you to the hospital."

"Don't tell Ray," Janet pleaded as Nick gave instructions into the receiver. "I don't want him to worry."

Nick hung up the phone and patted her hand. "Don't worry about Ray. I'll take care of him." He turned to Sarah, who hadn't moved from her position by the bed.

"You stay with her. I'll go down and unlock the door and turn some lights on so the ambulance will find us."

Sarah nodded, relieved that there was someone else to take charge. He reached out as if he wanted to pat her shoulder, but he stopped and turned away.

"I'll be fine," Janet told her, her voice tight with pain. "Now don't you worry, Sarah."

Sarah took her hand and held it tightly. "Sure you will. I'll have to tell the doctor you're getting married Friday, so he'd better work fast." She tried to smile. "After all, you still have to shop for your wedding dress."

Minutes after the paramedics entered the house and whisked Janet to the hospital, Sarah stood trembling in her bedroom, trying to focus on getting dressed as quickly as possible so she could follow the ambulance to the hospital. Losing Janet would be like losing her mother all over again. Only this time who would help her pick up the pieces? She took a deep breath and tossed a sweatshirt over her head. She was a grown woman, not a pregnant teenager. She could handle this alone.

THE DOCTOR CAME OUT to the waiting room and sat with them to explain that Janet's heart beat was irregular. He was transferring her to Intensive Care until her condition stabilized. He took one look at Ray and suggested he take it easy or they'd have another patient on their hands, and told them he would keep them posted. Sarah took Ray to the waiting room near Intensive Care while Nick went to the cafeteria. He returned with coffee and doughnuts, but Sarah only took one bite before realizing her stomach felt too tied up in knots for food.

"She gave me her engagement ring when the ambulance came," Sarah remembered, pulling it out of her pocket. "She was afraid something would happen to it in the hospital. Why don't you hold on to it for her, Ray?"

He took it, holding it carefully between his fingers. "I gave her another ring in 1944, for Christmas."

Nick leaned forward. "I thought you were in New Guinea then."

"I was. I sent my father the money and asked him to pick out a diamond for my girl." He tried to smile. "She wouldn't wear it on her left hand until I came back from the war, but she wore it, all right. Just knowing she wore it made me a happy man. I knew I could get through anything as long as I had Janet Fridrich waiting for me." His voice broke, and he rested his elbows on his knees and put his head in his hands.

Sarah swallowed the lump in her throat and put her arm around him. "Don't worry, Ray. She's going to be all right, I promise." She looked up and met Nick's worried gaze. Both of them knew she couldn't promise any such thing.

IT HAD BEEN the longest two days of her life, Sarah decided. They'd all taken turns staying at the hospital, going back to the house for a few hours of sleep when necessary. Janet's tests showed a blockage in one of the main arteries, and a specialist was called in to perform something called a "balloon" procedure, designed to open the blocked artery. The operation had been successful, but there was always the chance that the artery could collapse. They were keeping Janet in the hospital to keep an eye on her. Sarah kept Mary Anne and the rest of the family posted, but there was nothing anyone could do except wait. And pray.

On Wednesday morning the doctor announced that Janet was "out of the woods" and, as long as she continued to improve, could go home in a few days, along with her new medication and instructions to take it easy for a while.

"I'm not going to miss my wedding," Janet protested, propped up on pillows in her hospital bed.

Sarah couldn't help smiling. "You're just postponing it a few days, that's all. How does a New Year's Eve wedding sound?"

"No," Janet said, reaching for Ray's hand. "It has to be Christmas Eve. We'll be married right here, in the hospital. Reverend Neil won't mind performing the ceremony here, I'm sure. Right, Ray?"

"Anything you say, Peaches," he beamed. "Anything you say."

Sarah threw up her hands. "I give up!"

"Good," Janet beamed, still pale but smiling. "Nick, you take Ray home to get some rest. I want a few private words with my niece."

Ray kissed her forehead. "Good night, Peaches. Think about where we'll go on our honeymoon."

"I thought we already had one," she teased. "Isn't that what you told me in Denver?"

Nick opened the door. "Come on, Ray. Obey the lady's instructions and go home."

After they left, Janet turned to Sarah. "Now, the house is yours. It's in my will."

"Aunt Janet, please don't talk like that."

"Well, just in case, you need to know." Janet smiled, despite the oxygen tubes above her lip. "I don't plan to die for a long, long time."

"You've had us worried."

"I'm sorry. Do you think Ray is all right?"

"He'll be fine with one good night's sleep. And Nick is keeping an eye on him."

"He's a good boy. When are you going to marry him?"

Sarah hesitated.

"He's asked you, hasn't he? Ray told me Nick was going to."

"I can't, Aunt Janet."

The woman sighed. "Because of me?"

"Of course not." But Sarah knew as she spoke the words that Janet wouldn't believe her.

"I can't let this happen again, not to you," Janet cried. "You have to listen—"

The nurse came in. "You shouldn't stay much longer," she told Sarah. "We don't want our patient to get too tired."

"All right." Sarah started to leave the bedside, but Janet took her hand.

"Not yet," she pleaded. "There's too much to say."

"We can talk later, when you've rested."

"No. There might not be another chance. You need to know the whole story. Ray and I met in 1942, and wrote to each other all during the war. When he came back we were going to be married. Oh, he had plans for his father's store and plans for our future—he was something, that man!" Her voice trailed off, then she focused on Sarah's face once again. "I couldn't go with him. My mother was sick—we didn't know with what yet—and your mother and Mary Anne needed me. Father had died years before, so there were only the four of us, and the boarders, too. Aunt Esther was teaching in Chicago then and couldn't help me. So I stayed. Ray didn't understand, not really, but he went home and I was to join him when I could."

"But you didn't."

"No," she said sadly. "I didn't. We wrote back and forth for a few months, but nothing changed. After Mama died, I wrote to Ray and told him I couldn't leave my sisters. I sent back the engagement ring. I thought it was best that we each went on with our lives."

"And he never came back until now?"

"No. I never heard from him again, which I told myself was for the best. A few years after that I became engaged to a young man I'd known all my life."

"Uncle Jim."

"Your mother came to me before the wedding and confessed to taking the letters Ray had written after Mama died."

"Why would she do that?" Sarah remembered her mother as very sweet and undemanding, not the kind of person who would deliberately tamper with someone else's life.

"You have to understand. Louella had lost a father and a mother, and she couldn't bear to lose her oldest sister, too. She'd kept the secret for years, and then felt too guilty to let me marry Jimmy without knowing."

"What did you do? What did the letters say?"

"I didn't open them, Sarah. I didn't have the courage. And I thought the past was best left in the past. After all, it was years later, and I'd made my decision to stay in North Platte and take care of my family when I let Ray get on that train...."

"Poor Ray. He must have thought you didn't love him anymore."

"And I thought he was probably married, too. Don't do the same thing I did, Sarah. You're in love with Nick, it's written all over your face—and you've told him you won't leave because you don't want to leave me?"

Sarah tried to smile. "What are you, a mind reader?"

"His room is right above my bed, and there's nothing wrong with my hearing."

Sarah flushed. "I could never leave you, not after all you've done for me."

Janet shook her head. "You were the child I never had, Sarah. You reminded me so much of Louella then. You'd lost your father and your mother and you were so lost yourself."

"And pregnant."

"Yes. That, too." Her fingers tightened around Sarah's hand. "I gave up Ray because I needed to stay and take care of my sisters, but there was another reason." She took a deep breath. "I was afraid of leaving home, of leaving everything I'd ever known behind me. I didn't trust Ray's love enough. I wasn't very brave. And now I see you doing the same thing."

"Aunt Janet—"

"Hush. You're doing it, too—making excuses. Of course I'd hate to see you move so far away, but it would be worse to watch you stay here alone. I may not have that much time left. That's why I'm telling you this. Don't do what I did, Sarah. If you love Nicholas, don't let him go. You're afraid to tell him about the baby, you're afraid to trust his love for you. And that's wrong." Her blue eyes filled with tears. "Look at me and see what those fears have cost. And think about Nick. Do you want to wait another fifty years to see him again?"

FOUR NEWBORN BABIES slept behind the glass wall of the nursery. Three blue knit caps and one pink one covered their tiny heads.

Jenny had been born in this hospital, had slept peacefully while her mother made the decision that would affect both their lives forever.

Sarah knew it had been the right one. She'd been seventeen, too young to raise a child. Too full of grief and heartache to face the responsibility. Oh, she'd wanted to keep her baby, wanted to watch her blow out the candles on her birthday cake and shop for school clothes and take pictures of the prom. But Jenny deserved more than a teenage mother who hadn't even finished high school could give her. She hoped her daughter would one day understand.

She turned away from the babies and started down the hall. Nick headed toward her, his expression grim.

"Is it Janet?"

"No." he caught her in his arms. "She's sleeping, the nurse said. I took Ray home and came back for you." He looked past her to the nursery. "What are you doing up here?"

"I—" she began, but three days of unshed tears welled in her eyes. "Want to go home," she managed to say.

"Come here," Nick said, guiding her towards a plastic-covered bench against the wall. "Sit. This isn't the best time to talk about last night, but I've been doing a lot of thinking lately."

"Me, too."

He didn't look surprised. "I don't want to lose you, Sarah, but I know when to cut my losses and move on. I've looked at Janet and Ray these past months. Here they thought they had found each other again, and she's in the hospital and it turns out they've wasted a lot of years when they could have been together."

"But they're getting married."

"That's what I mean. Look at them. They're willing to do anything to be together, even in the hospital."

"I know. It's very... romantic."

"I'll wait until after the wedding, then I'll leave. I'm not going to buy the company, Sarah. I'll work something out with Ray that will give me distribution rights here in the West. I can work out of Denver, which is what I was trying to convince Ray of last fall." He took a deep breath. "I'm not going to ask you to move to Denver. I'm not going to ask you to marry me again. I am asking for an explanation, though. Just for me, the truth this time. Then I'm out of here, out of your life. I promise."

Sarah looked at him and her heart lurched. He was a wonderful, kind man who deserved an explanation, a real one. But would he hate her for it? Would he ever understand why she gave up her child, when he had grown up abandoned and unloved? But maybe Janet was right. Maybe it was time to face the ghosts of the past and let them go.

"All right." Still she hesitated, unsure where to begin. Finally, "Ten years ago, on Christmas Eve, I had a baby girl. Right here in this hospital."

She didn't look at him, unwilling to see his reaction. She rubbed the palms of her hands on her jeans, trying to restore warmth to her cold fingers. "I was seventeen. We lived east of here, in Grand Island. My boyfriend deserted me the minute I told him I was pregnant. And I had thought he loved me, of course. It wasn't a very happy time in my life. My mother had died the year before—heart problems, like Janet. My father was horrified to think I'd disgraced the family, so Aunt Janet stepped in and offered me a home. No strings attached. With the baby or without."

"Then what? You moved to North Platte, had the baby and what happened?"

The hard part. "I gave her up for adoption. To a young couple in Omaha who couldn't have children." She looked over at him, hoping against hope that he would understand. "I'm not ashamed of that, Nick. I gave her the best home I knew how. I just hope that someday she'll forgive me."

"Sarah," he said, his voice gentle, "why didn't you tell me before?"

"I've never told anyone. I wanted to tell you, but I couldn't bear it if you turned away from me, too. So I try to get through the holidays the best way I can, but I have a hard time on her birthday. I keep busy so I don't have time to think."

"And where do I come into this?"

"I didn't expect you," she admitted. "I didn't expect to fall in love again. I didn't want to change my nice, safe life and stir up all the bad stuff from the past." She shrugged. "I'm a coward."

"Not a coward, Sarah. But too hard on yourself. Don't you know how much I love you?"

"I didn't want to believe it. I didn't think it would last."

"Believe it, my love, even if you don't believe anything else." She didn't answer, so he continued. "Didn't you want more children?"

"I tried not to think about that," she said. "When you asked me to marry you I knew I couldn't leave my aunt. But I was really afraid to trust someone, afraid to love, afraid you'd hate me if you knew the truth."

"That's not fair, Sarah."

"It's how I felt." She turned to him, unaware of the tears that fell down her cheeks. "My boyfriend never spoke to me again, even denied the baby was his. My father didn't forgive me. Up until the day he died, he wouldn't look me in the eye. Not even after I graduated from college."

He took her in his arms and held her tightly against him. "I will love you forever," he promised. "Whether you marry me or not. I'll come back to your house once a year for the next fifty years and ask you to marry me. I'll put rings inside popcorn balls and quote Dickens and take you dancing and bribe you with hundreds of cookies until you say yes." He held her tighter. "Naturally I don't want to wait fifty years to make love to my wife, but I will. If I have to."

She pulled back in order to look into his eyes and see that he meant every word he said. The heaviness around her heart lifted, and she started to smile. "You mean it? *Hundreds* of cookies?"

"Of course," he said. "That's a promise."

Sarah put her arms around his neck. "What do you think the Ghost of Christmas Future would say is in store for us?"

"A lifetime of happiness, Sarah," he replied, his mouth finding hers. "What else?"

Epilogue

Christmas Eve,
Eight years later.

"READ IT AGAIN, Mommy," the little boy begged. "Especially the part about the ghost!"

Sarah shook her head and closed *A Christmas Carol*. "Not tonight. It's almost bedtime. Ask Grandma to read you one more very short story, and then you can hang your stocking."

"Come over here, Tim," Janet said, patting the empty space beside her on the couch. "What do you think Santa will bring you tonight? Did you make a list?"

"Yep."

Sarah looked at her watch. Santa was to arrive any minute, thanks to the enthusiasm of her next-door neighbor. His wife would ring the doorbell and "Santa" would walk through the yard, carrying a sack over his shoulder and calling for his reindeer. Last year Tim, only five, had fallen asleep before Santa's visit and missed the whole production.

"Where's Grandpa?"

"He and Daddy are in the kitchen." After Tim went to bed, the adults planned to celebrate Ray and Janet's anniversary by opening a bottle of champagne. Nick had added a guest wing to the house, hoping to encourage the older couple to extend their visits to Denver, especially during the harsh winter months. It was a plan that, to everyone's contentment, seemed to be working. The doorbell rang and Sarah hurried to answer it. "Why, I wonder who that could be!"

She opened the door, but instead of her neighbor, a pretty young woman stood under the porch light, fresh snowflakes dotting her chestnut hair. Behind her a taxi waited by the curb, its headlights muted by the falling snow.

"Mrs. Ciminero?"

Sarah nodded. The girl looked vaguely familiar. "Yes."

"Were you, I mean, are you—" The girl bit her lower lip. "Are you Sarah McGrath, by any chance?"

"Yes, I am."

"Who is it, honey? Should we look out the window?" Behind her Nick stepped to the door, holding a giggling toddler.

"No," Sarah said slowly. She almost dared hope, studying the young woman's hazel eyes. "Would you like to come in?"

The girl hesitated. "Maybe we could talk privately."

Sarah put her hand out, then stopped. She couldn't be sure, and she didn't want to make a mistake. "It's all right, really. Come in. Please."

Nick moved back, looking curiously from his wife to the young woman. Then realization dawned and he opened his mouth to say something, but stopped.

"I didn't mean to intrude," she said, "but coming here, meeting you, was my Christmas present from my parents." She flushed, as if she'd said the wrong thing. "We're in Denver for the holidays, and—"

"This is your eighteenth birthday," Sarah finished for her, realizing that once again Christmas was a time for miracles. Miracles and second chances. "Isn't it?"

"Yes. I'm Jennifer Ryan." She smiled suddenly, revealing a dimple in her cheek. "I think we've met?"

Sarah opened her arms and embraced her daughter.

A Note from Kristine Rolofson

Sometimes stories come to writers in the strangest ways. Years ago, when I discovered a Nebraska museum and its display of the North Platte Canteen, I learned that during World War II, the people of central Nebraska met every troop train and provided millions of service men and women with free meals, magazines and even birthday cakes. This Union Pacific stop in North Platte often meant the only good meal they would receive during the long cross-country journey. I thought it was terribly romantic.

When I returned to Rhode Island, I told my father about the canteen. His face lit up, and he said, "I remember..." His memories of North Platte hospitality led to other stories, including his regret over losing a World War II yearbook of the proud First Marine Division. With the help of an antique bookstore, I surprised my father with another copy of *The Old Breed*.

As I said, stories come in strange ways, and this one wasn't over. My father joined the First Marine Division Association, and soon afterwards a mysterious box arrived at his door. With no return address and a smudged postmark, it was filled with photographs, letters and mementos from my father's career in the navy. Where it had been and where it came from, I guess we'll never know.

But it makes me think that the world must be divided into two kinds of people: those who keep things and those who throw them away. Since I still have my 1964 Bob Dylan ticket stubs, all the letters my high school boyfriend wrote and my "McGovern for President" button, you know which kind I am. When it came time to write a Christmas legend for Harlequin, I chose to include the Ghost of Christmas Past...and a woman who saves a box of love letters for fifty years.

The man who loves her, a homesick medic off to join the First Marine Division in 1942, keeps his memories to share with another pair of lovers in Christmas Present, while the Ghost of Christmas Future promises happy endings to those who believe that love can never be forgotten. Tucked away in boxes or buried in our hearts, it surfaces at the most surprising times.

Wishing you a holiday filled with love.

When the only time you have for yourself is...

STOLEN moments ™

Christmas is such a busy time—with shopping, decorating, writing cards, trimming trees, wrapping gifts....

When you do have a few *stolen moments* to call your own, treat yourself to a brand-new *short* novel. Relax with one of our Stocking Stuffers—or with all six!

Each STOLEN MOMENTS title is a complete and original contemporary romance that's the perfect length for the busy woman of the nineties! Especially at Christmas...

And they make perfect **stocking stuffers**, too! (For your mother, grandmother, daughters, friends, co-workers, neighbors, aunts, cousins—all the other women in your life!)

Look for the STOLEN MOMENTS display in December

STOCKING STUFFERS:

HIS MISTRESS Carrie Alexander
DANIEL'S DECEPTION Marie DeWitt
SNOW ANGEL Isolde Evans
THE FAMILY MAN Danielle Kelly
THE LONE WOLF Ellen Rogers
MONTANA CHRISTMAS Lynn Russell

HSM2

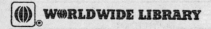 **WORLDWIDE LIBRARY** ®

HARLEQUIN®
Temptation®

If you missed any Lovers & Legends titles,
here's your chance to order them:

Harlequin Temptation®—Lovers & Legends

#425	THE PERFECT HUSBAND by Kristine Rolofson	$2.99	❑
#433	THE MISSING HEIR by Leandra Logan	$2.99	❑
#437	DR. HUNK by Glenda Sanders	$2.99	❑
#441	THE VIRGIN AND THE UNICORN by Kelly Street	$2.99	❑
#445	WHEN IT'S RIGHT by Gina Wilkins	$2.99	❑
#449	SECOND SIGHT by Lynn Michaels	$2.99	❑
#453	THE PRINCE AND THE SHOWGIRL by JoAnn Ross	$2.99	❑
#457	YOU GO TO MY HEAD by Bobby Hutchinson	$2.99	❑
#461	NIGHT WATCH by Carla Neggers	$2.99	❑
#465	NAUGHTY TALK by Tiffany White	$2.99	❑
#469	I'LL BE SEEING YOU by Kristine Rolofson	$2.99	❑

(limited quantities available on certain titles)

TOTAL AMOUNT	$
POSTAGE & HANDLING	$
($1.00 for one book, 50¢ for each additional)	
APPLICABLE TAXES*	$
TOTAL PAYABLE	$
(check or money order—please do not send cash)	

To order, complete this form and send it, along with a check or money order for the total above, payable to Harlequin Books, to: *In the U.S.*: 3010 Walden Avenue, P.O. Box 9047, Buffalo, NY 14269-9047; *In Canada*: P.O. Box 613, Fort Erie, Ontario, L2A 5X3.

Name: _____

Address: _____City: _____

State/Prov.: _____Zip/Postal Code: _____

*New York residents remit applicable sales taxes.
Canadian residents remit applicable GST and provincial taxes.

LLF

Earth, Wind, Fire, Water
The four elements—but nothing is
more elemental than passion.

Join us for

Four sizzling action-packed romances in the tradition of
Romancing the Stone and *The African Queen*. Starting January
1994, one book each month is a sexy, romantic adventure
focusing on the quest for passion...set against the essential
elements of earth, wind, fire and water.

On sale in January
To melt away the winter blues, there's *Body Heat* by
Elise Title, bestselling author of the Fortune Boys series.

To win the hot role of an arson investigator, movie star
Rebecca Fox knew she had to experience the heat of a
real-life investigation. So she sought out the best one in
the business—Zach Chapin. Soon Rebecca and Zack were
generating more heat than the torch they were tailing.

The quest continues...
Coming in February... *Wild Like The Wind* by Janice Kaiser.

Passion's Quest—four fantastic adventures,
four fantastic love stories

Travel across Europe in 1994
with Harlequin Presents and...

As you travel across Europe in 1994, visiting your favorite countries with your favorite authors, don't forget to collect four proofs of purchase to redeem for an appealing photo album. This photo album can hold over fifty 4"×6" pictures of your travels and will be a precious keepsake in the years to come!

One proof of purchase can be found in the back pages of each POSTCARDS FROM EUROPE title...one every month until December 1994.